Kyra Kyralina

Panaït Istrati

Kyra Kyralina

translated by
Christopher Sawyer-Lauçanno

Talisman House, Publishers
2010 • Greenfield • Massachusetts

The translation and publication of this work is generously
supported in part by the Romanian Cultural Institute, Bucharest.

10 11 12 13 14 7 6 5 4 3 2 1 FIRST EDITION

Published in the United States of America by
Talisman House, Publishers
P.O. Box 896
Greenfield, Massachusetts 01302

Manufactured in the United States of America
Printed on acid-free paper

ISBN 10: 1-58498-075-3
ISBN 13: 978-1-58498-075-9

The cover illustration, from a painting by R. Jeandot, appears with the
permission of the Monik Benardete Collection, Istanbul.

Book designed by Samuel Retsov

Translator's acknowledgments: I am deeply indebted to Edward
Foster, Robert Couteau and Patricia Pruitt for their careful reading,
comments and suggestions on my translation. They have made this a far
better English version than it would have been otherwise. I also want
to thank Pierre Zoberman and Carmen Firan for their support of
my translation. Any faults are my own.

The publisher is grateful to Monik Benardete, M. Özalp Birol, and
Nilgün Mirze for their help in the preparation of this book.

Contents

Romain Rolland, Preface . . . 1

Panaït Istrati, author's note . . . 3

Book I: Stavro . . . 5

Book II: Kyra Kyralina . . . 39

Book III: Dragomir . . . 77

Translator's note . . . 137

Panaït Istrati . . . 139

Romain Rolland

Preface

In early January 1921 a letter arrived for me from a hospital in Nice. It had been found on the body of a desperate young man who had slit his throat. There was little hope that he would make a recovery. I read it and was seized by the tumult of genius, like a wind burning on the plain. It was the confession of a new Gorki from the Balkans. They managed to save him. I wanted to get to know him. We began corresponding. We became friends.

His name is Istrati and he was born in Brăila in 1884, the son of a Greek smuggler whom he never knew, and a Romanian peasant and remarkable woman who vowed to work ceaselessly to raise him. Despite his affection for her, he left home at the age of 12, possessed by the demon of the road but even more by the desire for knowledge and love. For 20 years he wandered. His adventures were extraordinary: exhausting work, ramblings and pain, in which he was burned by the sun, soaked by the rain, homeless and harassed by night watchmen, hungry, sick, passion-possessed and broken by misery. He did just about everything: cabaret waiter, pastry chef, locksmith, tinker, mechanic, manual laborer, stevedore, house boy, sandwich man, sign painter, house painter, journalist and photographer. He even mixed himself up for a while in revolutionary movements. He wandered through Egypt, Syria, Jaffa, Beirut, Damascus, Lebanon, the East, Greece and Italy, often penniless, stowing away from time to time on ships. When discovered in mid-route, he was forcibly put off at the nearest port. Although destitute, he has stored up a world of memories, and often appeased his hunger by reading voraciously, mostly the Russian masters and Western writers.

He is a born storyteller, a teller of Oriental tales, and once he launches into a story, no one knows, not even him, if it will last an hour or a thousand and one nights. The Danube and its meanders... His genius for storytelling is so irresistible that even in the letter he wrote me the evening before his suicide attempt, twice he interrupted his desperate account to narrate two humorous stories from his past life.

I helped him to decide to write down some of his stories and he is now engaged in a long work of which two volumes are actually written. They are evocations of his life; and the work, like his life, should be dedicated to friendship. For this man, friendship is a sacred passion. All along his route he finds himself stopping to recall faces he once encountered; each one bears the enigma of destiny that he seeks to penetrate. And each chapter of the novel is also a short story. Three or four of these, in the volumes I've read, are on a par with the Russian masters. But he differs from them in temperament and light, the turns of the intellect, a tragic gaiety, and the joy of telling a tale about the oppressed soul.

One should also remember that the man who wrote these lively pages only began to learn French seven years ago by reading our classics.

Panaït Istrati

You have been advised by our dear friend Romain Rolland that I should devote some lines of explanation of the general theme that runs through all my books.

I never thought that I would be required to explain a few things about this subject. I am not a professional writer, and never will be. It was only by chance that I should have been plucked from the vast ocean of society by that fisherman of men from Villeneuve (Rolland). I am his work. So that I could live my second life, I needed his esteem, and the only way I could obtain this warm and friendly esteem, he told me, was by writing. "I do not expect exalted letters from you," he wrote me. "I expect books. Create works more essential than you, more lasting than you. You are only the seed." With this whip cracking over my back—and also thanks to the oats of friendship offered me so generously by my friend George Ionesco—I trotted off with a spring in my step. The stories of Adrien Zograffi owe their existence to us three. Alone, I would have been incapable of doing anything other than house painting, taking landscape photographs and other ordinary work that anyone could do.

Adrien Zograffi was nothing at first but a young man in love with the Near East. Self-taught, he finds his Sorbonne where he can. Later, he will dare to say that a good many things have been poorly made by mankind and the Creator. I know it is very dangerous to criticize the Creator as well as the men who do not paint houses or take shoddy photographs of the Promenade des Anglais, but as they say in France it is impossible to please both the world and its Father. I hope, above all, that you will pardon Adrien's audacity, for in taking advantage of his freedom, he is permitting himself another audacity, that of loving and of being, always, everywhere, a friend of those who have hearts. There are few of these, but Adrien does not think that humanity is as vast as commonly thought.

While awaiting his story, you will first need to listen to the stories of others. Please listen with him.

Book I:
Stavro

Adrien wandered in a daze along the short Boulevard of Mother-of-God, which in Brăila extended from the church of the same name to the Public Garden. At the garden entrance he stopped, confused and vexed.

"All the same!" he exclaimed in a loud voice, "I'm no longer a child! And I know I have the right to live my life as I feel I should.

It was six o'clock in the evening. A day's work was over. The garden paths near the two main entrances were nearly deserted, and the setting sun gilded their sand, while the lilac bushes were plunged into evening shadow. Bats whirled directionless, as if in distress. The rows of benches lined up along the pathways were almost empty except for a few secluded ones in the corners where young couples were linked together only to right themselves when someone inopportunely passed. Adrien did not pay attention to anyone who crossed his path. He deeply inhaled the pure air rising from the freshly watered paths, took in the multiple fragrances of flowers, and considered his difficulties that he wasn't able to sort out. Most of all he could not understand his mother's opposition to his choice of friends, objections that had just led to a violent discussion between his mother and her only son. Adrien tried to figure it out: "For her, Mikhaïl is an outsider, a suspicious worthless servant of Kir Nicolas, the pastry cook. But why? Who am I, myself? I am a housepainter, and before I used to be the servant of the very same pastry cook. And if tomorrow I went to another country would folks there necessarily consider me worthless?"

Angry, Adrien kicked the ground. 'My God, it's terribly unjust to poor Mikhaïl. I like that man because he's more intelligent than I am, more schooled, and because he endures misery without complaining. How? If he refuses to shout his name to the rooftops, his nationality and the number of teeth he's lost, he's nothing better than a worthless guy? Well, as for me, I swear that I'm going to be this no good's friend. And I feel I'll be glad because of it.'

Adrien mechanically continued his walk, all the while mentally turning over his criticism of all that his mother had said, and all that seemed to him absurd. "And this whole thing about marriage? I'm not yet eighteen and she's already thinking of saddling me with some fool of a woman or maybe some little bunny who will smother me with tenderness and turn my room into a cesspool. My God! One might think that there is nothing more intelligent to do on earth than to produce little imbeciles, to fill up the world with slaves and to become slave number one of this vermin. No, no! I'd love much better to have a friend like Mikhaïl, even if he were at times more suspect. As for pulling people's tongues to make them talk, I'm not quite sure why I like to do it. Maybe it's because light shines out of the speech of strong people, as God proved when he spoke before there was light."

The strident horn from a boat pierced the calm spring evening, turning Adrien's musings elsewhere, as the scent of roses and carnations wafted over him.

Adrien wandered to the grand promenade that borders the plateau and overlooks the Danube and the harbor. For a moment he stood still to gaze at the thousands of lights that beamed from the boats anchored in the port, and he felt rise in his chest an irresistible desire to travel. Lord! How fabulous it would be to find oneself on one of those boats that glide over the seas, and to discover new shores and new worlds.

Depressed by the knowledge that he could not give in to his desire, he walked on with his head lowered until someone called to him from behind, "Adrien!" He turned. A man was sitting on a bench smoking, his legs crossed. Adrien was nearsighted, and in the darkness he could not make out who had called. The man did not rise, so Adrien approached him somewhat ,ly. Suddenly Adrien cried with delight, "Stavro." They shook hands, and Adrien sat down beside him. Stavro, the itinerant peddler, commonly known as "the lemonade seller" because of the concoction that he sold at fairs, was a second cousin of Adrien's mother. He had once been a familiar figure in the gay circles outside the city. But he was now forgotten, buried under thirty years of history and the fallout from a scandal for which his temperament had been responsible.

A little taller than average, with dirty blonde hair and pale skin, he was wrinkled and thin. His large blue eyes, sometimes frank and sincere, sometimes scheming and furtive, depending on the circumstances, told you who he was. His life had been topsy-turvy and rough since he had turned twenty-five because of his nomadic and bizarre nature. At that age he was caught up in the whirling gears of a sad marriage to a rich, beautiful and sentimental young woman from whom he extricated himself a year later, covered with shame, his heart in pieces, and his character warped.

Adrien knew the story vaguely. His mother, without providing details, had told him the tale as an example of an odious life. But Adrien had come to a conclusion quite the opposite, and more than once he had been drawn to Stavro as one is drawn to a musical instrument whose resonance one wishes to hear but that refuses to make a sound.

They had met three or four times at the most, always outside. Adrien's mother's house was closed to Stavro, as were all honest houses. After all, what could an itinerant peddler have to say to a little lad so well cared for and doted on as Adrien, who was the focus of his mother's attention?

Stavro was regarded by everyone as a boaster, which in fact he was and wanted to be. His clothes were tattered and worn, even when new. He looked like a citified bumpkin with his wrinkled collarless shirt. His cascade of words, accompanied by a slew of gestures, was delivered like a horse dealer's or horse thief's. And while his listeners found his torrent amusing, his words were not without considerable bite.

He would greet acquaintances on the street by calling them names that were accurate and comical, though never ones that angered. Many of these nicknames stuck. If he liked someone, he would take him to a café, order a half liter of wine, and after some conversation find a reason to excuse himself, never to return. And when someone he encountered began to bore him, he would tell the person, "Your friend is waiting for you in such and such a café. You better go."

But what most enchanted Adrien were Stavro's tzir or heads of red herring, and his tobacco box con games. In the course of a conversation, Stavro would fetch from his pocket one of these little dried and splayed fish heads, with its mouth wide open, and would surreptitiously fasten it to the back of the victim's jacket. Afterwards, the guy would saunter along the streets with the head seeming to bite his back, much to the amusement of onlookers.

The tobacco box joke was even better. In the Near East the custom is that if you want to roll a cigarette, you ask to borrow a friend's tobacco box. Stavro never missed an opportunity to ask the first person who showed up for his tobacco box. After he had taken what he wanted, instead of returning the box, he would put it in his own pocket where immediately it would fall out and roll to the ground. He would then pick it up, wipe it, beg forgiveness, and then, while attempting to return it to the pocket of its owner, would drop it again. By now the poor box—made of nickel or cardboard—would be much the worse for wear. "Oh, how clumsy I am." "It doesn't matter, sir," would be the invariable reply of the mystified owner as he examined the beat up box in Stavro's hand, while the onlookers burst into laughter. And, of course, Stavro never returned the beat-up boxes to their owners.

Adrien had begun by liking Stavro because of his games. But from time to time there were strange things that bothered and confused Adrien. Occasionally, in the middle of some stupid antic, Stavro would become serious and gaze intently at Adrien. His look was calm yet superior, his eyes not unlike those of an innocent calf. This would make Adrien feel small. But Adrien was also fascinated by the outcast. Since what happened seemed inexplicable, Adrien began observing Stavro more closely, but he rarely saw this sudden transformation. When he did observe this mysterious and troubling gaze, Adrien took to calling him secretly "the other

Stavro." But not often did Stavro adopt that look, and he never looked at anyone except Adrien that way.

Then one day, about ten months before the meeting in the Public Garden, he had accompanied Stavro to his spice merchant, a taciturn old Greek who supplied the lemonade seller with sugar and lemons. Suddenly Adrien saw "the other Stavro." There were just the three men in the corner of the poorly-lighted shop. Adrien looked over and saw Stavro's wrinkles recede, his features soften, and his wide-open fixed bright eyes focus on the old grocer. Stavro then spoke rather timidly but firmly while the other nodded approvingly: "Kir Margolis. Things are going poorly. It's never hot and the lemonade won't sell. I'm eating up my savings and your sugar. Do you get it? This time, again, I can't pay. OK? It'll be like the other times. If I die you lose ten francs."

The merchant, though very tight with money, knew his man, so he extended credit, settling it with a shake of his dry little hand.

Outside, with the parcels under his arm, Stavro cracked a joke, slapped someone he hardly knew on the back, and began to dance about on one foot. "I pulled a fast one that time, Adrien, I pulled a fast one," he whispered into the young man's ear.

"No you didn't, Stavro. You'll pay up."

"Sure, Adrien, I'll pay if I don't die. If that happens, the devil will pay."

"If you die, well, that's different. But you said you pulled a fast one. That means you're dishonest."

"Perhaps I am."

"No, Stavro you're putting me on; you're not dishonest."

Stavro stopped suddenly, then pushed his companion back against the railing, and for an instant his face took on the look again, and he spoke with the same mix of temerity and force. "Yes, Adrian, I am dishonest. Unfortunately, very dishonest."

That said, he wanted to take off, but Adrien, in a sort of panic, took hold of the lapel of his jacket, and cried weakly, "Stavro, don't go. You've got to tell me the truth. There are two Stavros. Which one is the real one: The good one or the cheat?"

"I don't know."

He brutally tore away Adrien's hands.

"Leave me alone!" he yelled angrily. Then, after a few steps, realizing he'd upset the young man, he added, "I'll tell you which is which when you finally get your nose unstuck."

They hadn't seen each other since. Stavro sold his lemonade outside of town from March to October, and during the winter he peddled, when he could, roasted chestnuts. He only came to Bršila to restock.

Adrian was as happy as a river that flows into the mouth of the ocean and then disperses into the breast of distant seas when he met up with Stavro that day on the bench in the Garden. Adrien was pleased that on this occasion Stavro was far less loquacious than normal. He looked at the face of his friend in the yellow evening light and found him the same as usual. No one could have said how old Stavro was but Adrien did notice that along his temples his pale blonde pale hair had become smoky white.

"Why do you look at me like that?" he said, somewhat annoyed. "I'm not for sale."

"I know, but I want to know if you are still young or already old."

"I'm young and old, like the sparrows."

"It's true. You are a sparrow, Stavro." Then, after pausing he added, "Do you want to repeat your old joke and drop me on the floor? I'm always curious to know where you've come from and where you're going and how your business is coming along."

"Where I've been and where I'm going is not important but I can tell you that my business isn't too bad. I am a bit upset today, though, my little man." He tapped Adrien's knee.

"You don't get mad very often, do you? What's the matter, old man? Are lemons becoming hard to get?"

"No, it's not the lemons that are hard to find. It's 'honest rogues.'"

"'Honest rogues?'" exclaimed Adrian. "That's a contradiction. Rogues can't be honest."

"You think so? I've known quite a few." Stavro reclined on his haunches and looked at the ground. Adrien sensed the seriousness of his talk and wanted to draw him out but he proceeded prudently.

"Can you tell me what favor it is that you want somebody to do for you?"

"To accompany me to the fair in S. next Thursday. It's not really for me but like this. You know that at the fair I always set up next to a pastry seller who makes crepes. The people eat, get thirsty, and there I am with my lemonade; if need be a little bit of salt can be tossed into the crepes. (You see how dishonest I am.) And well, I have the pastry man—Kir Nicolas.

"Kir Nicolas," exclaimed Adrien.

"Yes, your neighbor, your old boss. But the trouble is he can't leave his oven and come to the fair. That's why I need an honest rogue to go with his servant, Mikhaïl. He'll collect the coins while the crepes are cooking in the oil. I've been looking for an honest rogue for two days."

Stavro concluded gravely and sadly, "Brăila is becoming poorer and poorer in people."

Adrien was taken aback by the tale. He stood before the lemonade seller and said: "Do you think I'm worthy to be the honest rogue you seek?"

The outcast raised his head. "Are you joking?"

"I give my word as an honest rogue that I'll go with you!"

Stavro leapt up like a chimpanzee and whooped. "Give me your paw, you son of an amorous Romanian and a roving head case. You are a worthy descendent of your ancestors."

"What do you know about my ancestors?"

"Well, come on. They had to be great rogues."

The lemonade seller embraced Adrien, then took him by the hand, and began to lead him. "We have to hurry to Kir Nicolas's house to tell him the good news. We leave, at the latest in the afternoon, tomorrow, Sunday, so as to get to the fair in S. by Tuesday morning and get ourselves a good spot to set up. The trip takes one day and two nights by cart. The horse goes at his own pace, according to how strong he's feeling; our pace is determined by the quality of the wine served at the inns.

The apparition of the fair master and his new "boy" occasioned an animated discussion at the pastry shop. Kir Nicolas understood through Stavro's excited talk that Adrien had been bought. Stavro, protesting, delivered a long tirade in Turkish until he ran out of breath, and Mikhaïl, who knew what had actually happened, injected himself into the dispute, to Adrien's great astonishment, who did not understand a word. After Mikhaïl had gotten his say in, Adrien saw Kir Nicolas shrug his shoulders.

Stavro, now somewhat calmed down, nonetheless shouted in perfect Greek, "Don't get so worked up about what his mother will say. If I had lived my life for the last fifty years as my mother had wanted, I wouldn't have known anything more than that the sun rises and sets over the ditch that surrounded our beautiful city of Brăila; You see, my friends, mothers are all alike. They want to relive in their children all their little pleasures and their charmless boredoms. And besides, I tell you, we can't be blamed for the faults we were born with. Right, Adrien?"

Mikhaïl intervened again, in Greek. "You're right in principle, but we don't know Adrien's mother. I propose that we send Adrien to ask her permission. If she says yes, I'll be the first to cheer. But if she says no, then I'll refuse to go to the fair."

This sent Adrien off like the wind. His mother was in the kitchen preparing dinner when he arrived. He stopped in the middle of the room, his eyes wet, and his cheeks red. He had not decided in advance what he was going to say, and so he hesitated before he could speak.

But his mother saw that he had gone mute, and quickly began to speak herself. "You've got your head in the clouds again."

"Yes, mother."

"Well, if you're going to serenade me with the same old song, make it quick. Do what you believe you need to do without breaking my heart too much, and don't get too concerned about me. It's better that way."

"But this isn't about something heart breaking, mama. I've been without work for eight days, maybe more, and I want to go with Mikhaïl to the fair in S. It will be a good opportunity for me to visit that beautiful country and at the same time pick up the cash I'm losing."

"Are just the two of you going?"

"Yes. No. Stavro's going, too.

"Oh, that's nice. This gets better and better. Your 'philosopher' too is going."

And over the silence of her son, she added, "All right. You can go."

"Without you getting mad, mama?"

"Without me getting mad, my friend."

They were ready to depart that Sunday, under the watchful eyes and joking mouths of all the merchants on Grivitza Street, neighbors of the pastry maker. Stavro arrived about four in the afternoon, with his cart and provisions, including his water jug and lemonade barrel along with sugar, lemons, and glasses. In front of the pastry shop with the help of Kir Nicolas and Mikhaïl, they loaded on the equipment for making crepes: a table, a little stove, a large crepe pan, two sacks of flour, quite a few oil tins, and utensils. They also attached a seat on which the three of them could sit.

To spare Adrien from the jibes of the onlookers, his mother and he had left a half-hour before Stavro's arrival; they had headed up Galatz Street, her, toward the house of a friend, he toward the Grand Route near where the cart would pass.

She embraced her son, and said, "Look, Adrien, I bow to your wishes but one day you will regret your actions. The little journey that you are making today will give you a taste tomorrow for longer trips and later even longer travels. And if you can't guarantee my happiness in the future, I'm certain we will both end up in tears, which will not please God."

Adrien wanted to speak, but she had gone. Unable to move, Adrien followed her with his eyes. She walked as straight and narrow as her life had been: simple and sorrowful. The one thing she had done wrong she did not regret even though it had cost her dearly. With her scarf over her head and her bargain blouse, her handkerchief in her right hand, she held up her long skirt with her left hand so it would not drag in the dirt. She fixed her eyes on her feet as if she were looking for something—not something she'd lost, but something she was soon to lose.

Adrien, my poor brother! You tremble. In that cart burying itself in the ruts of the federal road, you are curled up on the cushion. On one side is Stavro, who guides the horse at a trot while singing songs in Armenian, and on the other is the silently smoking Mikhaïl, whose shoulder presses into you. You tremble, my brave friend, but not from the cold. Do you tremble from fear? Or is it being seated between those two demons who've entered your life that gives you the chills? Is it the breath of destiny pushing you not only to the fair at S. but also toward the great fair of your new life?

For a long time, a very long time, under the reflection of a twilight sky that promised a storm, they traveled along the road that stretched out like a rope dividing the fields from the forest. All the while Stavro sang and lamented his fate in Armenian. For a long while Mikhaïl and Adrien listened without understanding a word but sensing everything. The night enveloped them leaving each to his own thoughts. Villages and hamlets followed one after another, miserable nests of sadness and happiness, swallowed by shadows and ignored by the universe. In the flickering light of the lantern, swinging back and forth from the cart, nocturnal visions of the rustic and pitiable towns rose up for an instant only to disappear: a dog barking furiously; the corner of a curtain pulled back at a window where a person peered out; old thatched roofs battered and blackened by spells of bad weather; pathways between crumbling walls.

Every two hours or so Stavro stopped at an inn, rubbed the horse's eyes, pulled its ears, held a grain bag under its mouth, covered it with a blanket, then noisily followed his companions inside. In the tavern he would become boisterous and high spirited, cracking jokes, telling wild tales, and from time to time, giving a friendly tap to a peasant's hat. After he had ordered "a liter of wine for himself and a glass for the bar owner," he'd politely ask the bartender for his tobacco box, roll himself a cigarette, then under the guise of thanking him, would drop it to the floor.

Adrien noticed that Mikhaïl, who had only known Stavro for a couple of days, was watching him discreetly but constantly. Taking advantage of a moment when Stavro was not present, he said in Greek to his friend, "What a rogue. So much talk with nothing being said." He then added, "It's babble intended to make everyone else silent, but I don't know why. In any case, he's got something to hide."

Around midnight, after seven hours of traveling, almost always at a brisk pace, and fatigued, with a light rain beginning to fall, they arrived in the village of X where nothing was distinguishable except a pack of raging epileptic dogs that attacked the horse. Stavro whipped at them cruelly and guided the cart with precision toward a door that entered into a courtyard. The horse pushed it open with his head, almost breaking it off its hinges. From his seat, Stavro shouted at the inn's window, "Gregoire! Hey, Gregoire!"

After a long wait a black silhouette came to open up, and agitated, Stavro yelled, "I swear, by all the holy saints and apostles, do you want me to make crêpes and lemonade with the rainwater? Open up quickly, you damned cuckold!"

The cursed innkeeper grumbled something back, and took the horse by its bridle. He removed the bit and bridle, and parked the cart. The three travelers and the innkeeper hastened into the inn where they found themselves in a Romanian room like that of Uncle Anghel, where one eats, drinks, smokes, and talks about good or evil things depending on who is there, and how old they are, and how good the wine is.

Stavro was brief. "Let's eat well, and not waste our time talking. We'll set off again at dawn. The hardest part of the trip is behind us. Tomorrow morning, when we're rested, we can tell stories all we want as we travel alongside the river and watch the sun rise right in front of the horse's eyes. It's going to be beautiful tomorrow."

Clinking glasses with Stavro, the innkeeper asked, "Are you going to the fair in S.?

Stavro nodded, and the innkeeper began to tease him, "Are you still making your lemonade with saccharine instead of sugar, and citric acid instead of lemons?"

Stavro looked straight at him, then after chewing his mouthful of food, said, "And you, you animal, are you still making your eau-de-vie to poison the peasants and increase your profits out of alcohol and fountain water?"

Adrien, astonished, interrupted, "But Stavro, I saw you buy sugar and lemons; weren't they to make lemonade?"

"No, my friend, they were just eye candy to fool the thirsty." He then added, in Greek, "You see how dishonest I am. And that's nothing. I can be far worse."

Mikhaïl and Adrien exchanged knowing glances, and with their eyes communicated their understanding that Stavro had much to hide.

The three men got up. The innkeeper gave them a box of matches and a candle, and took them to the hay loft half filled with straw. A large mat was laid out on the floor, on which all three of them tumbled, undressed, their stomachs full, a little dizzy from wine and fatigue.

"If you smoke, be careful," the innkeeper told them as he took back the candle and matches and left. Five minutes afterward the three were asleep.

What time could it have been? Adrien couldn't say but at a certain moment in the dark night he had felt a hand touch first his shoulder, then his face. Upon opening his sleepy eyes, he was at pains to remember that he was not at home but on a farm. He fell asleep again, but again the hand began moving over his face and he felt a hot kiss on his right cheek. This time Adrien woke up completely, but remained still. What the devil did this mean? Blinking in the dark, he recalled where each was sleeping: to his right and in the middle was Stavro; on the other side of Stavro was Mikhaïl. And he thought, "What? Is Stavro kissing me? What's going on?"

An idea planted itself in his brain, so awful that he shook it off, "No. I've got to be dreaming. It's not possible!"

But within a few minutes, he again felt Stavro's hand stroking his chest over and over. Frightened, he called out in a strangled but deep voice, "Are you joking with me?"

The question resonated in the calm night as if intoned inside a bell. Jumping up, the lemonade seller grabbed his arm and trembling with emotion whispered into Adrien's ear, "Shut up!"

"But what do you want? Weren't you the one who just kissed me?"

"Shut up. Don't shout," Stavro said under his breath, as he continued to clutch Adrien's arm.

After a few seconds, Mikhaïl punctured the frightful silence by quietly asking Stavro something in Turkish. Though not wanting to answer, Stavro mumbled a few words in response. Mikhaïl renewed his questioning. This time Stavro replied at length. And again, after Mikhaïl had pressed him hard, Stavro drily answered. Mikhaïl thought about what Stavro had said for a moment, then propping himself up on an elbow, looked straight into what he took to be Stavro's eyes and spoke to him calmly for a minute or so, this time without interrogation. But in the middle of Mikhaïl's speech, Stavro angrily cut him off. And then something happened that filled Adrien with terror.

Mikhaïl, whom Adrien had never known to be violent, leapt up and began shouting loudly. Stavro replied in kind, now upright himself. The two began violently arguing, though what they were actually saying was lost on Adrien. In the pitch black night, words struck against words, as if they were swords in the hands of fencers. Adrien could hear only their movements but could imagine their heads nearly touching, their eyes uselessly trying to see, their arms swinging. Adrien, frozen in place, listened to the din of Turkish vowels resonating like oboes, and the numerous hard consonants raining down like drum rolls.

The truth finally dawned on Adrien just as Mikhaïl seized Stavro in a vice grip. Adrien, overcome with pity for Stavro, burst into tears. Wailing, he called out, "Speak Greek. I don't understand a word you're saying."

This explosion of grief ended the quarrel. A heavy silence fell over Adrien's words broken only when Adrien cried out, "Stavro! Why did you do that?"

Stavro turned to Adrien, and answered, his voice weak, "Well, my poor friend, it's because I'm very dishonest. I told you that."

Mikhaïl, now calm, interjected, "It's worse than dishonesty. It's perverse. It's violence against harmony and tranquility. You poisoned the air with your vice. The worst crime of all is to spread your perversion. Apologize sincerely to Adrien. If you don't, I'm out of here. You can have your fair to yourself."

Stavro didn't say a word. He rolled a cigarette, and when he lit it, the two others could see his that his face, in profile, was unrecognizable. He was ghostly pale, his mouth and his nose elongated, his mustache bristling. His eyes were sunken, and he didn't look at them, even when they themselves rolled their own cigarettes and lighted up.

Outside the barking of dogs and the crowing of roosters pierced the night air.

"Yes," Stavro said, after a long silence, and well after Mikhaïl had given up hope of getting a response. "Yes, I'll sincerely apologize to Adrien. Sincerely but not humbly. But only after you've heard what I have to say."

"You say 'perversion,' 'violence,' 'vice.' And you believe that I'll be sunk in shame. I've already told you that I'm dishonest. And to be dishonest is really the worst of all since as I understand it being dishonest means you are consciously doing wrong. My good Mikhaïl! These things you mention are done every day, all around us, and no one revolts! They are forgotten by the law, are in our customs. They've become a way of life. And I'm a victim of this perverse life. Everything in my life has been made of perversion, violence and vice. I grew up breathing them. Nonetheless, I've never been inclined toward them. I hate to have to speak about this but it's easier when we're wrapped in night like the moles in their kingdom. I'm not telling you this to defend myself; that doesn't matter. I'm doing this because this immoral man wants to give you moral folks a lesson about life. Particularly you, Mikhaïl, who think you know more than you do, you need to listen.

"I'm an immoral and dishonest man. As for my dishonesty, I don't have excuses. But the immorality, I'm the only one who can judge it. You'll see why when you hear about the adventure of my marriage.

"In 1867, a little after Prince Charles took over these lands, I too returned to my country, but not like a prince. I came back crushed by the loss of my older sister, and corrupted by the life of adventure I'd led for twelve years in search of her throughout Armenia and Turkey. Unfortunately for you I can't begin the tale with my childhood, or recount the tragic story of my sister, or tell you how I became perverted. It's much too long a tale. Maybe one day, if you still want to know me, I'll tell you. And if you don't want to hear it, that's fine with me, too.

"I had just turned 25 when I returned. I had a little money, and knew three Eastern languages. I had almost forgotten my Romanian by then. My childhood friends didn't know who I was, but this didn't bother me as I didn't want to know them anyway. Besides, I even had papers saying I was a *reaya,* or Christian Ottoman subject. And since I spoke my language poorly, I passed as a foreigner.

"Why did I come back to my country? For nothing and for something big. For nothing, because I had no roots in the soil where I first saw life, and besides, I liked living in foreign countries. However, I wasn't totally committed to being abroad. I lived a free life, nomadic, but corrupt. My only experience with women involved my sister and mother. I'd never had a wife or even a mistress. And I wanted so much to have one, but I was filled with fear about acquiring one. That's something you don't know anything about, Mikhaïl. Oh, how many wrong ideas we have. When people see a man who has lost his leg or arm, they don't reproach him, everyone has pity for him. But no one has pity for a man with a crippled soul. But it's really the pillar of life he's lacking. No one respected me. I returned to Romania to get support from those whose morals were more ordinary. They gave it to me, but just when I had begun to benefit, they abruptly withdrew, shamefully throwing me back into a life of perversion.

"Upon my arrival, I returned to my old calling of *salepci,* selling hot salep root flour drinks at markets and fairs outside of Brăila, and even well beyond. No one in town knew what I did for a living. I bought the salep secretly from a Turk, who believed me to be his countryman, and to whom I confided only what I wished. In this trade I worked little and made a fair amount of money, using only the extra I carried in my waist belt to get by. And then I began to make friends.

"Dressed as a *chiabur,* or a man of leisure, I bought flasks of wine here and there for any and all. One day, in the old outlying area of Brăila, the Oulitza Kalimérsque, I happened upon a very good wine. At the same time, I discovered what I had been seeking since my return—now almost a year past. The wine was served by a beautiful *crâsmaritza,* or bar maid, who was the owner's daughter. I became a regular drinker of this fine wine, all the while becoming the prey of the flashing black eyes of the one I idolized. But I was prudent: the family was austere but very rich. Moreover, they didn't like foreigners, even though they owed their fortune to them. Knowing this, I hastily got my Romanian papers, an easy task in countries where Saint Bakshish reigned supreme. One day I was Stavro, the salep peddler; the next I was Dumnul Isvoranu, a Damascine copperware merchant. My name and my trade went over and I began to get regard and attention from the family. The mother was dead, the father was old and severe, and suffered from leg problems.

"After three months of frequenting the place, one evening I was invited to dinner with the family. There I was introduced to an aunt who had replaced the mother, and who smothered her niece with affection. In talking about myself, I was careful only to lie by halves. Also at the table were her two brothers, as large and strong as *gdéalats*—Turkish executioners. As it turned out, they were also in the Damascine rug and copper business, at Galatz. Fortunately, I was better acquainted with Damascus and their trade than they were as I also used to sell carpets and copper goods from there.

"During the meal I told stories and recounted scenes about life in Anadolu, making sure that I laid stress on how exploitative it was for those who made Damascus carpets and copperware. I pointed out how everything was made by five-year-old children or else old folks nearly blind. The kids earned only two *meteliks* a day, or about a cent; they barely knew what it was like to be a child, and entered life through the doorway of torture. The old folks became less and less able to work each day and never had the right to rest nor enjoy the serenity that should be present in old age.

"My lighter stories amused the young lady and the sadder ones made her cry but the others had hard hearts and only took in the anecdotes. This so annoyed me that I was on the verge of drawing back but then I remembered that I was not interested in marrying the whole family. The daughter happily showed me that she felt the same as I, and she was the only one I wished to marry.

"Within two months from that first dinner I had become an intimate part of the family. The house had few visitors, and its atmosphere was stifling, but the only one who was bothered by it was the happy girl I loved. Every night I would spend two or three hours with her, telling witty stories, and from time to time singing plaintive but melodious oriental songs. The aunt and the father found them pleasant enough but the daughter was infatuated with them and wanted encore after encore.

"In the shop, the father did not tolerate noisy behavior and quickly chased out any raucous patron, which is why few ever opened the door to ask for a drink. The family was ensconced behind the shop. The aunt kept house, washed the clothes, and checked on the shop through a partly open curtain that veiled a glass door. The young woman embroidered or made lace, while the father stretched himself out on a bed in the alcove, dozing, occasionally groaning as he listened to me. He was dumb as a sheep, and when I sat on the sofa next to him, and laid out my plans, he believed everything.

"I quickly discovered his weak point: he was in need of a resourceful man to continue his business, and he saw in me just the one to do that. Everybody knows that few Romanians take to business; they are merely slaves to the earth. But as he wanted to give his daughter away to a businessman with some knowledge of trade, and since at that time the easiest customers to manipulate with success were foreigners, he was quite content to have found a man of the world who spoke several languages and who could counsel his sons, who were as stupid as he was. Indeed, until I learned that their mother was a businesswoman of the first order who had left money behind, I often wondered how these brutes had managed to make small fortunes. The daughter had her mother's temperament; but after her mother's death no one did what he did not want to do.

"My appearances made the air fresh and all five breathed it in deeply. The old man and the two sons, who came every other Sunday, acted like idiots and suffocated me with their questions about business, always about business. When they wanted proof of my honesty, nothing more intelligent occurred to them than to ask me for some money, and then later on entrust me with some of their own. I satisfied them in both cases, thinking to myself that stupidity and money were twins. In that, the three of them hardly differed.

"The old aunt, the mother's sister, did not laugh, and cried even less. She frequently grilled me about my present business. For a while I deflected her questions but she began to be suspicious. Knowing that I had the confidence of the three imbeciles, I finally gave her a long explanation about how for the last couple of years my business had not been doing well due to a lack of capital. It was only half a lie; had I had more money I could have done quite well since at that time the foreign copper business was the one to be in. And besides, I had never said I had a lot of money.

"What filled my heart with joy was the beautiful Tincoutza's attachment to me. Only she understood me and loved me; she alone inspired me, and gave me hope in that house of hopelessness.

"I was a free man who cared nothing for money. I was used to breathing in the brisk winds of life that whisked away nature's miasmas. I wouldn't have lingered in that house where everything was degraded because of self-centeredness and stupidity except for her whose only fervent aspiration was for freedom.

"Frequently we were left nearly alone. At nightfall the shop was closed and the aunt went to bed as she got up early. Tincoutza sat next to her father, and one could never know, even through his moans, whether he was sleeping or not. One evening, bent over her embroidery, in a tone that turned my blood to ice, she asked, 'Tell me some story, Mister Isvoranu, something sad.'

"'No, not sad. Those tales bore me,' interrupted her father.

"'All right, then tell a happy one,' she said in a melancholy tone.

"'I'll tell one that will appeal to all tastes,' I said. 'Last year I found myself at a fair on the banks of the Jalomitza River. You know that at a fair the only wise thing to do is to treat everyone well. In life you make friends quickly and dissolve friendships just as quickly, but one peddler runs the risk of running into another peddler more often than a dead man meets the priest who buried him.'

"'Say, that's clever,' the old man muttered.

"'I followed that code of conduct of being nice to everybody, and this is what happened. I'd known for a short time a peddler named Trandafir, a gypsy who pretended to sell glass bead necklaces but really was in search of easy dupes to rope into a three-card monte game called 'Here's the King, Where's the King?' To be honest, Trandafir was a grifter, but he interested me. With his necklaces draped over his arm, he stopped in front of my stall speechlessly smoking his pipe; then after every exhale would spit. He so disgusted me that I was ready to send him away. But before I could kick him out, he went into the crowd crying out, 'Necklaces, necklaces.' His eyes followed the heads of the peasants in order to find clients for his game, whose pockets he could empty. Wanting him to make his living more honestly, I suggested to him once that he change his profession.

"'What?' he asked me. 'You want me to go in with you?'

"'No,' I said. I can't make you my partner, but I can make you into a salep seller. You'll make pretty good money.'

"'Oh sure. Pretty good money. Your salep would never make me enough to give my beautiful Miranda a new ducat for her necklace every six months. And if I didn't, old man, she'd set out to find another, for love, you know, is fickle.'

"I told him he was right. Salep doesn't produce ducats the way three-card monte does. And just that afternoon he'd made five ducats worth twelve francs each from his cards. And a quite funny story goes with those five ducats. A young peasant who'd been conned wasn't taking it lightly, and the two of them, after a long crazy chase through the fields, arrived at my stall, asking me to arbitrate.

"The peasant spoke first: 'If he won't return my money, he should teach me his profession, yes, his profession, so I can do what he does.'

"Trandafir shrugged his shoulders. 'He's a fool and a pain in the ass.'

"'No, old man,' said the peasant. 'My money or your trick. It's not worth being honest. I want to do what you do.'

"'But you're no more honest than I am," yelled Trandafir. 'You wanted to win my money, but I was sharper than you and I won yours. That's the whole story.'

"'Yes,' agreed the peasant. 'I wasn't much more honest than you, and for that I'll let you have one ducat but give me back the other four. If you don't, I'll throw myself into the Jalomitza River, and that's a sin. I have a young wife home alone. We are full of love for each other. And those five ducats that hung from her necklace were all we had. I was on my way to buy two horses and work the earth.'

"Trandafir jumped up as if burnt by a red iron. 'What? Imbecile, you took your wife's ducats to buy horses? Oh, you don't deserve a wife with a ducat necklace.'

"'But what am I to do?' lamented the young man.

"'What to do?' yelled the gypsy. 'Go five leagues away from your house and steal the horses but leave the ducats hanging around your wife's neck.'

"And turning to me, Trandafir, said, 'Have you ever seen a Romanian as stupid as this?'

"Having said this, he became rather thoughtful, smoking and spitting. The peasant cried, holding his hands to his face. And then to my amazement, Trandafir turned toward the young man, yanked his hands away from his face, and as quick as lightning, slapped him twice.

"'Why are hitting me?' implored the young man.

"'Because you're stupid. And I don't like men who cry,' said the gypsy, rolling his coal black eyes like a devil. 'Here are your five ducats. Now go back home tonight, but at sunrise stay within gunshot range of the high road that passes outside the village. I'll bring you your two horses, and I'll even give you two more slaps to help you remember never to touch a beautiful woman's ducat necklace except to enrich it.

"Six months after this incident I ran into Trandafir on the road to Nazîru. He was on horseback and I was in a carriage. As we passed each other, I asked him if he'd kept his word.

"'Yes,' he replied. 'I gave him the two horses and the two slaps.'

"While I told my story the father was sleeping, but Tincoutza was more moved than ever. It was then I realized that for the first time in my life, I was alone with a beautiful woman who looked at me with loving eyes, a little teary, sparkling with passion. She leaned toward me, took my hand and said in a voice sweeter than the chord of a violin, 'Tell me, Mister Isvoranu, could you love me like the gypsy Trandafir?'

"I couldn't say whether her hand burned or was ice cold, but I do know that I was seized by a sudden panic. My head swirled as if I'd fallen off a roof, and without further ado, I grabbed my hat and left.

"She thought it was some joke on my part, and laughed heartily about it when she saw me the next day. But I was in despair: my fear of finding myself alone with a woman manifested itself more than ever. All the hopes I had had pinned on those few months of intimacy vanished. I remained as I had been: a man with a contorted soul.

"Meanwhile, as they do with horses afraid of fire, I began sticking my nose in the flames believing that I would end up losing my fear of her. And who knows? What do we know about human nature? Less than the beasts do! Perhaps had I had the leisure to quell my perverted senses, my instincts would have become more primitive, and I would have had success in achieving a balance. But for this to happen, I would have had to possess the goodwill of my fellow men and the benefit of circumstance. Neither the first group nor the second was willing to rescue a poor man like me. Circumstances made me a poor man, while my fellow men couldn't see beyond the self-centeredness that ruled them. The result was that we all crashed our heads into the wall, and the one who suffered most was me.

"I did not want to ask for Tincoutza's hand before I was certain that my nature was at least beginning to feel somewhat different. But another player put the situation in danger. Tincoutza fervidly announced that she would marry no one but me, and her father asked me what I thought.

"What could I think about it? Even the idea of marriage threw me into all the terrors of hell! I couldn't say anything. I was evasive, confused. Tincoutza, her pride offended, burst into tears, and I felt my gut wrenching within me. Her father attributed my confusion to the fact that I was not a rich man, and in consoling me he said, 'You will be rich one day working here.'

"Can you believe it? He actually thought it was his money that I was after.

"Thus, with the chasm approaching, I went straight to him and asked for Tincoutza's hand. She was thrilled, and the house awakened from its lethargy. But I felt lost. The days that followed my proposal began to resemble the last moments of a man condemned to death.

"Tincoutza was beside herself. 'It's your emotions that have so beaten you down,' she said to me one day. 'I am so happy.'

"Poor girl, I thought.

"To numb my senses I played the fool from morning to night, but it was obvious that I wasn't like I had been before, and on the evening of my betrothal I was on the verge of fainting. The family was quite intrigued by my state as was my fiancée, but they thought I was simply overwhelmed by emotion. They urged me to talk, to tell a tale. I ransacked my brain for something to say but came up with nothing. But a priest who had come to exchange rings and bestow the blessings of the church on us, gave me an idea. He was going on about field work and complaining about how his farm hands were deliberately slow workers. I said, in order to set up my story, 'If you want them to work faster, father, there's only one way.'

"'What's that, my son?'

"'To swear, swear like a *surugiu*—a coach driver.'

"'Ah but we can't swear; it is a sin to do so.'

"'Yes, I know it's a sin, but I know of a man who was absolved for swearing by the archbishop of Bucharest, since there was nothing else he could have done.'

"The priest looked skeptical, but the rest urged me on.

"'How? Please tell us. Tell us how.'

"'Well, it happened this way. One day the archbishop of Bucharest needed to go to a town for an official ceremony. The finest coach arrived, and his Holiness climbed aboard. But the coach driver was quite unhappy despite the tip promised him. Everyone, of course, knows that a coachman can't drive his horses without swearing. For him, cracking a whip and swearing is even more important than a big tip, but worried about angering the Archbishop, the *surugiu* sealed his lips and drove silently, as well as he could for three hours. But arriving at the ford of a river he stopped short. His choking back curses had turned him red as a cooked crayfish. He threw down the reins of his four horses and decided to reclaim his right to swear at any cost. The Archbishop became impatient with the wait and, sticking his head out of the coach window, demanded to know why they had stopped. The coach driver removed his hat and humbly explained, 'It's that, you see, Very Highest Holiness, the horses are used to the *surugiu* swearing at them. But as I can't swear in your Holy Presence, they don't recognize me, and therefore refuse to ford the river.'

"The Archbishop responded, 'Well, my son, shout at them. Giddyup! Giddyup! My bold horses!'

"The cunning coach driver repeated almost under his breath the words of the Archbishop. But the beasts didn't budge.

"'Isn't there any other way besides swearing at them to get them to move?' asked the Archbishop, quite impatiently.

"'No, holy father. To tell you the truth, horses won't march without oaths and curses.'

"'In that case,' said the Archbishop, 'go ahead and curse them and I'll absolve you of sin.'

"The coach driver bounded from his seat, retrieved his reins, cracked his whip, and shouted in a voice that would have frightened dead men,

'Giddyup! Giddyup! By the sacred slippers of the Virgin! By all the holy icons! By the fourteen gospels. By the sixty sacraments. By the twelve apostles and forty martyrs of the Church! Giddyup! Giddyup! My bold horses! In the name of God and the Holy Spirit!'

"The carriage glided like a swallow across the ford. Once on the other bank, the archbishop again stuck his head out the window, and told the triumphant driver, 'That was amazing how your horses responded, but you are quite lacking in religious education. There are not fourteen gospels, only four; and there are not sixty sacraments, only seven.'

"'Yes, of course you're right, Holy Father, and I know that. But see here: the numbers four and seven are far too small to curse the way one should. We coachmen need to arrange our religion to fit our professional requirements.'

"This story provoked much laughter but embarrassed the priest. I, however, felt much more at ease. Tincoutza was radiant and proud of me.

"Ah, if things had only remained like that. Or why hadn't I rescued myself before the drama unfolded? For the drama, interminably long, arrived three weeks later—three weeks of unprecedented torture, hardly credible, when each kiss from my sweetheart seemed like warnings to get my legs in motion and lose myself in the world. The tragic drama began with the nuptials.

"Now I've come to the monstrous contract that shattered my life and that of the innocent Tincoutza. I've arrived, my good Mikhaïl, at your perversion, at violence or vice, at all the maledictions that brutes who walk on two legs practice in the form of customs, of traditions that poison life and tyrannize innocents. For, along with my chaste fiancée, I also was an innocent, though in my case one with a sickness.

"Perhaps, Mikhaïl, you don't know of what I speak. You don't know that with us, on the wedding night, the women of the family and even women who were not related, invade the bridal chamber a few hours after the young couple have retreated there. They tear the bed apart for irrefutable proof of the young bride's chastity, proof that they carry in triumph to show those invited to the banquet gathered in the room next door. And I've even seen worse: I've seen these sheets carried like a flag on a pole by a maniacal mob who screamed and shouted beneath their awful trophy all the way along the road from Petroï to Cazassou. At dawn, on this Monday, they were accompanied by a gypsy who scratched the strings of a fiddle. And they continued carrying this blood-red sign until they reached the door of the happy mother of this poor girl.

"Do you know anything, Mikhaïl, more barbarous or abominable? Is perversion or perversity, rape or violence, vice or sadism more inhumane, crueler and more outrageous than this hurtful and haunting practice?

"I knew all about this when the day of my wedding arrived. It wasn't just the custom that I found revolting. But at that dangerous hour when I knew my sensuality would betray me without pity, it was in my own vital interest to send this despicable masquerade to the devil.

"I called the father and aunt together to talk with them. The father, though he loved this repugnant custom, was not so set on it; the old aunt, on the other hand, was insistent on having the custom respected, as if it were a tradition of the country, a guardian of honor.

"That settled it, and the wedding went forward on a beautiful Sunday afternoon. At the church there was the necessary ostentation: everyone came on foot except for two horsemen in front. They were followed by a man who carried, on a huge engraved silver platter encrusted with gold, two gigantic Moscow candles, and after him the wedding party. On exiting the church, the horsemen, with long scarves tied to their arms, again led, firing pistols. The horses, their manes braided with ribbons and silver, pranced. On the silver platter now was the customary bread and salt. I followed immediately after, gripped by fear and misery. I had a candle in my hand and a delighted Tincoutza on my arm, practically hidden under her elaborate heaps of finery. Behind us came the wedding attendants, including twelve musicians who played their violins, cobzas, clarinets and cornets deafeningly. Some women returning from the town well poured their jugs onto our feet to wish us good luck.

"And that night, the fateful bell tolled for me. There was a table set for twenty guests, including the family. The prayers offered by the well wishers put everyone in a good mood, and I had to put on a festive face and exchange stories with them. One of the guests, his brain warmed by wine, had the bad taste to recount how in his village a young bride had been found lacking by her new husband, and as a result, on their wedding night he had beaten her. The next morning he tossed her in his cart, her back to the oxen, facing the rear where he had balanced on the end of a stick an earthenware pot with a smashed bottom. Like this, he took her back to her terrified parents.

"I looked at Tincoutza. She remained calm, sure of her innocence. But I was startled by the story, and shouted that what took place between two married people was solely their business.

"'We'll see a little later whether it's nobody else's business,' said several of the guests.

"The words 'a little later' meant that. As the clock struck twelve midnight, I felt little balls of bread striking my face, then larger pieces, then finally chunks of bread being hurled at me from all directions.

"'What's this about,' I demanded.

"'It's time to get up from here and go do your duty' cried the godmother.

"I swear to you, my friends, that I had no idea what she was talking about, but I finally understood what I was supposed to do after the godfather took me aside. While he spoke to me, Tincoutza's godmother and aunt took her into the bedroom to pretty her up; they then emerged from the room and hugged me. Her father opened the door to the bed chamber and they all pushed me in, then closed the door behind me.

"That moment was one of the worst of my life. I vaguely recall seeing my bride's lovely head on the pillow with her black hair spread out around her, but that's all. Right in the middle of the room I keeled over in a dead faint.

"A high fever left me delirious for twenty-four hours, and I was ill for fifteen days. I have no idea what I may have said while unconscious, but I do know that few came to visit me. When I recovered I found myself in enemy territory. My father-in-law and the aunt demanded explanations for the dishonor I had brought down on the family. Since I knew the popular belief that witchcraft could make a man impotent, I saved myself temporarily by claiming that I was under some kind of spell.

"From that moment on, and for the next ten months, I was circled by hate and hostility. I was excused from family events; I was not given any sort of role in the business. They kept their money tightly shut up as if I were a thief. To take care of myself I could do nothing but revert to being a salep seller, since I had spent nearly all my savings on wedding gifts. And so began that terrible life that even now frightens me when I recall it.

"I can't recount every detail of my existence; it was too awful. Barricaded in the miserable house I didn't even dare to put my foot into the street except rarely and only at night. I was barred from the shop. No one came to visit me; I had no work. No matter what I proposed, it wasn't accepted. At the table we sat like deaf mutes. In slippers and shirtsleeves I walked from room to room like a parasite or a fool.

"My two brothers-in-law came every Sunday. I asked them to take me into their business at Galatz since I knew something about it. They talked of divorce. And that truly would have been the wisest solution. But it couldn't be.

"During our marriage my wife was completely detached from her family. Her whole life now revolved around my miserable and crippled existence. Without tears or rancor she had accepted, with inconceivable bravery, our misfortune, believing that I truly was under a spell. She fervently prayed to the good Lord to vanquish the devil and cure her husband whom she loved despite his weakness.

"We closeted ourselves, conversing interminably, and ventured into degrees of tenderness I'd never known. I begged her forgiveness. She responded that there was nothing to forgive. Oh, how can I ever forget the only human being who understood me and who had taken pity on me? And who can tell whether, without the hatred that poisoned us, I might have become the husband and run-of-the-mill kind of man that I so fervently desired to be? Already I was less timid than at the beginning of our relationship. I no longer was afraid of my wife, and even better, my blood no longer froze at her caresses. There were even moments when vague desires, weak awakenings, small sexual impulses formed in my body and made me turn red when, enclosed in her arms, she caressed me, assuring me of her love.

"But that which love creates with difficulty, hatred can destroy in an instant, and that's what makes me unable to forgive mankind. Each morning, just after I had left my room, the two horned owls who presided over our misfortune would swoop down on my poor wife to ask if anything had happened. At her refusal to speak, these two devils would advise her to separate from me and would continue torturing her until she was in total despair.

"This constant hammering and systematic destruction of the little that nature had tried to rebuild went on for ten months. We were suffocating. The two hangmen from Galatz started to become quite aggressive toward me, insulting me and insisting that I give up my wife. There was nothing to support us. We huddled together, often even refusing to go down to eat, managing to get by on one meal a day, and mulling over how we might save ourselves.

"She asked me if the little money I had left could support us. I replied passionately, describing how freedom and love would be hers once we had distanced ourselves from this moribund house. At this, she burst into tears of joy. Joined like two brothers lost in enemy territory, we bathed our faces and even our clothes in tears, and we lived the happiest hours that I have ever passed on earth.

"But these hours were also to be the last that we would ever have together. The great wave of the men's hatred was about to inundate us.

"By the end of February we had hatched our plan. We were going to wait a month, and toward the end of March, we were going to board a steamer bound for Stamboul.

"But not long after we'd made our decision, we began to notice a definite change in the attitude of the two tyrants: they suddenly ceased pouncing on my wife each morning, they no longer terrorized her, and the old man even told me that I could go in and out of the house as I pleased. I was knocked over. I ran to Tincoutza, but she dissolved into tears.

"'I feel evil is hovering,' she said. 'I saw you in a dream last night surrounded by crying children, and I was decked out in gold and precious stones. It is awful. Don't go out! Who knows what might happen? We've been imprisoned for ten months; we can endure it for a few weeks more.'

"These words sent a dagger into my heart and I startled to tremble. But man's fate is written in advance. The dawn the next morning was beautifully still. More than a foot of snow covered the world in an immaculate white shroud, and sleigh bells filled the air with their nostalgic sound. I stood at the window and it seemed as if the walls of the house vanished around me. An irresistible force called me outside where there was movement and life and the spontaneous mystery of a free existence that I had not known for almost a year. I threw myself at the feet of my wife and pleaded with her to allow me to go out for an hour, a half hour, five minutes, beyond the walls and roofs and misery.

"She listened to me and gave her permission but advised me to take my knife and two pistols, and implored me not to talk to anyone. I kissed her slippers, put on my fur coat and cap, and went downstairs to the shop.

"Ah, that was my undoing, and also that of Tincoutza! Our demise did not happen instantly, for nothing happened to me that morning nor that afternoon nor the next day. But on one of my walks I was seen by a traitor whom my father-in-law had ordered to hide behind the wall of the shop and spy on me.

"Returning from my walk on the evening of that last Sunday that I lived in that house, my eyes full of the majesty of the Danube on which ice sheets floated, I kissed for the last time she who had for the past ten months been the most tender wife and the purest of virgins.

"We were calm. But when we came down for dinner we could feel the weight of tragedy bearing down on us, setting us on the verge of tears. Toward the end of the meal, Tincoutza asked, 'Why aren't my brothers here?'

"'They'll be here later,' replied her father.

"We lit our hookahs and drank Turkish coffee. Outside was night and silence. It began to get late. Suddenly, Tincoutza noticed the two old folks exchange a knowing glance, and she burst into tears.

"At that very moment the door swung open, and the two brothers, as somber as executioners, entered. In their wake was a man whose appearance made the blood drain from my face. It was a Greek who used to be my friend but who had become a criminal.

The three stood in the open door. The traitorous Greek spoke first. Raising his arm and pointing at me, he said in Romanian, 'Is that him, your Mister Isvoranu? I understand he's bewitched. Well, that's Stavro, the salep seller, and the only thing wrong with him is that he's a queer.'

"At that word, which named both my vice and his, Tincoutza began to wail and roll on the floor, while I, a victim of the cruel vengeance of my two brothers-in-law was dragged out of the shop. They whipped my feet, beat my head and my face, and punched me in the stomach, only stopping apparently when I was unconscious.

"When I came to I found myself in the snow in front of a bolted door that led to a closed passageway into a courtyard. I had no winter clothes, no hat, and I was shivering, nearly frozen. My limbs, my stomach, and my head were bruised and bleeding.

"I gathered all my strength and went to ask for help from a Turk who had furnished me with salep root flour eighteen months before. He received me like a Christian and took care of me as if I were his brother.

"Four days later, the good man, who had no idea to whom he was speaking, brought to my bedside the news that had been making the rounds of the town that morning: Tincoutza had been fished out of the Danube by some fishermen.

"Since then thirty-five years have gone by, and each year on that fatal date I go to the banks of the Danube with its floating ice sheets and beg forgiveness from Tincoutza for what I did to her.

"'And Adrien, I also ask your forgiveness for what I did to you just now.'

Along the road to X., between fields of rye, the cart with its three men trundled along at a good pace. Above the head of the horse, who snorted in the fresh morning air, the shepherd's star of the Levant twinkled in the purple canopy of light. A lark soared out of the field like an arrow bound for heaven.

Stavro watched it until it began to descend like a pebble, his eyes fixed on the place where it had disappeared, and began to sing a song composed in that universal language known by men the world over who have no homeland, and whose melody was never written on paper:

If I were a lark
I'd glide in the blue sky
But I would never swoop down to earth
Where men sow wheat
Where men reap wheat
Where they sow and reap without ever knowing why…

Book II:
Kyra Kyralina

When the cart carrying the three wanderers had stopped for lunch in the grove, Stavro refused to bend the ear of his companions, who for an hour had pleaded with him to recount the story of his and his sister's childhood that he had evoked at the beginning of his tale in the hayloft. It wasn't that he didn't feel like talking about it—he was now completely disposed toward recalling the distant past—but a little coaxing helped to open the sluice gates holding back the waters of the past.

They stretched out on the moss under the trees, smoking cigarettes, while the horse grazed on the grass and sniffled as it picked its way around them. Stavro got up, piled up some dry branches and lit a fire; and when the coals were ready, he rummaged through the cart for the coffee utensils, boiled the water, and tossed just the right amount of coffee and sugar into the copper *ibrik*. After which, with the talent of a Turkish coffee master, he poured the foamy, aromatic liquid into the three saucerless cups, called *félidganes*. He then served it, and sitting back on his haunches in Turkish fashion, began:

"I don't remember the date or my exact age at that time. But I know that the event that followed after that dramatic episode was the Crimean War. As a small child I recall the hardness of a father who beat my mother everyday without any reason that I could understand. My mother was often absent from the house; he would beat her before she left and when she came back. I never knew if the mistreatment before she left was so that she would leave, or so that she would return, nor on her arrival, whether it was because she had left or come back.

"I also remember that at that time, now fogged in memory, next to my father sat my brother. He was the first born and as hard as my father.

I felt great attraction for my sister Kyra, who was four years older than I, and whose existence was nearly as awful as my mother's.

"Bit by bit the fog of memory dispersed. I grew up and began to understand, and there were some very odd things to understand. I was probably eight or nine, my sister thirteen and so beautiful that I spent my days as close to her as possible in order to see her from head to toe. She admired herself, as did her mother, who was as beautiful as her daughter. In front of the mirror, sharing an ebony makeup box, they would do their eye lashes with *kinorosse* mixed with oil, their eyebrows with a twig of sweet basil wood charcoal, while they colored their lips and cheeks with red *kirmiz*, as well as their fingernails. And after this long operation, they kissed one another, exchanged tender words, and set about getting me ready. Then the three of us would join hands and dance Turkish or Greek style, all the while pressing kisses on each other. We were a family unto ourselves.

"During this time my father and older brother didn't come home every night. They were both wheelwrights, and the best and busiest in the region. Their house and workshop were on the other side of town in the Karakioï Quarter, while we lived in Tchétatzoué. Between us was the whole town. The Karakioï house belonged to my father. He had two apprentices who boarded and roomed there, as well as an old servant who took care of the house and them. We never went to his house, and I barely remember the shop, which frightened me on account of my father. On our side of town, in the house that belonged to my mother, we spent our days enjoying each other and life. In winter we drank teas, in summer syrups, and all year round we ate Turkish cakes like *kadayif* and *sarailie,* drank coffee, smoked hookahs, put on makeup and danced. It was a good life.

"Yes, it was a beautiful life, except on the days when my father or his son, or the two of them, would burst into the middle of our festivities to beat my mother unmercifully, and punch Kyra with their fists, and break their sticks over my head, since I was also dancing. As we spoke Turkish fluently, they called the two women *patchaouras*, or whores, and I got called *kitchouk pézévéngh,* a little pimp. The two ill-treated women would fall at the feet of the tyrants, their legs crossed, and beg them not to hit their faces, 'Not our faces! In the name of the Savior and the Holy Virgin, don't hit our faces! Don't hit our eyes! Please!'

"Ah, their faces, their eyes, the beauty of the two women! No one on earth could have put up with this. They had long blonde hair that fell to their waists, fair skins, and their eyebrows, eyelashes and pupils ebony black. Though their ancestral tree was Romanian on my mother's side, three different races were grafted together: Turkish, Russian and Greek, since these groups had all dominated the country in the past.

"When my mother was sixteen her first child was born, but at the hour when I opened my eyes no one would have believed her to be a mother of three children. And this woman who was made to be caressed and kissed was instead beaten until blood ran. And while my father did not waste his caresses on her, her lovers compensated brilliantly. I've never known whether my mother began to deceive my father and got beaten for that, or if my father's maltreatment caused her to be unfaithful. In any case, the drama never ended in our house. Cries of pleasure alternated with cries of pain; and not long after the thrashings were over, smiles again lit their tear-soaked faces.

"I mounted guard and ate cakes, while the well mannered and even decent clients sat Turkish style on the rugs, singing while the women danced. They played tunes of the East on a guitar with a castanet and a tambourine for accompaniment. My mother and Kyra, dressed in silk and devoured by pleasure, danced with scarves, turning, pirouetting until they were dizzy. Then, their faces enflamed by the heat, they would throw themselves on large cushions, tucking their legs and feet under their long dresses, and fan themselves. Fine liquors were served, and incense burned. The men were young and handsome. They were always brown or black and elegant with their pointed mustaches and trimmed beards. Their hair, straight or curly, exuded a strong scent of almond oil or perfumed musk. They were Turks, Greeks, and also, but rarely, Romanians. Their nationality did not matter, as long as the lovers were young and handsome, delicate, discreet and not in a hurry.

"My role was thankless. I have never told anyone until this moment how much I suffered then. My job was to be on the lookout, seated on the window sill, and to warn of any surprises that might be on the way. This pleased me well, for I hated to death the men of Karakioï who beat us. But within me a terrible battle raged between my duty and my jealousy. I was horribly jealous.

"The house was situated at the back of a large walled courtyard. The front windows overlooked the courtyard, while those in the rear gave onto the plateau above the harbor. No one could enter the house except through the front, but to be sure, to make a hasty retreat, it was easy to leave through the back. If the strip of land behind the house could have spoken, it would have told tales of men tumbling down the slope.

"I crouched at the window, my eye fixed on the lantern that shined on the gate, my ear cocked for the sound of rusty hinges rustling. I also kept an eye on the festivities inside. My mother and Kyra were beautiful enough to drive anyone mad, with their corseted waists nearly small enough to fit through a wedding ring, their swollen breasts like two melons, their sumptuous hair flowing over their naked shoulders and down their backs. Red ribbons served as headbands, and their long eyelashes fluttered diabolically as if to kindle the jets of flaming desire that shot from their eyes.

"Frequently in their attempts to please the women, the guests got so wound up they seemed ridiculous. One evening one of them said to my mother, 'Old chickens make the best soup.' The poor woman was so vexed by the remark that she threw her fan at the man's head and began to cry. Another of the guests rose up angrily, thumbed his nose at his rude companion, then spit in his face. A furious fistfight erupted. Tables and hookahs crashed to the floor. The more they went at it, the more we laughed. My mother finally restored the peace by embracing them both. But these hugs and kisses served another purpose as well. A sweet voice, a clever phrase, a pretty game ensured that rewards were returned to her. She used all her wiles to turn bad moods to good, to erase an ill-spoken word, to calm the fury of a jealous lover, to placate an idiot.

"Kyra also excelled in her own way. Though only fourteen, she was so physically well developed she could pass for sixteen or older. Giddy but cunning, with her button nose, prominent chin, and two dimples that God had placed almost symmetrically on her cheeks, Kyra couldn't charm both her lovers and me with her mischief, her jokes, her little games; her lovers wanted to get the upper hand, and I felt she gave them too much.

"We called the clients by the Romanian term *moussafirs,* or guests. And these *moussafirs* kissed her hands and her sandals whenever they could. She would pull them by their noses or their beards, pour syrup on the glowing ashes in their hookahs. She would offer them a drink from her glass, then to tease them would break it just as they got it to their lips. But a moment later she would be dabbing a cut lip with a strand of her hair.

"All this put me into a rage, for I loved Kyra even more than my mother. I adored her and could not put up with anyone caressing her except me. One evening my misery was pushed to the breaking point. The tie on her sandal had come undone during a dance and she placed her foot on the knees of a *moussafir* and asked him to relace it. You can imagine what an opportunity it was for this lucky devil. He took as long as he possibly could in order to prolong his pleasure. But I was watching him like a wolf. The creep began to stoke her ankle and even her leg. And she, well, she didn't say anything, she let him do it! Finally, furious, I lost my head, and yelled out, "'Father's coming! Save yourselves!'

"In the blink of an eye, the two *moussafirs* jumped through the windows and disappeared in the dark, rolling down the slope. One of them, a Greek, in his haste forgot his fez and guitar, but my mother picked them up and threw them out the window after him. Kyra busied herself by rapidly hiding the extra hookahs.

"This scene was so funny that my anger quickly disappeared and turned to hysterical laughter. I slid from the window sill, rolled back and forth on the carpet, laughing so hard that I turned purple. My mother thought that I'd gone insane out of fear of my father, and both of them pierced the air with their startled cries. In their concern for me, they forgot about that devil, my father; they hovered over me, in total despair.

"'There's no father!' I finally managed to say. 'I was just angry because Kyra was allowing her leg to be stroked. And I took my revenge.'

"The joy at this news made them shout even louder. They pounded my butt, all the while hugging and kissing me. We then all began jumping around the room. They were happy to be alone and unscathed, and I had been pummeled less than I'd been hugged.

"We went along for two or three years like this. These are the only years of my childhood that I can remember clearly. I was eleven, Kyra fifteen, and I was inseparable from her. Later, I realized that that it was desire that so attached me to her. I followed her everywhere like a dog, spying on her while she did her toilette, and kissing the clothes impregnated with her scent. The poor girl weakly but tenderly defended herself from my attentions as she believed me to be an innocent and not in the least bit dangerous. To tell the truth, I was not aware of any particular intention. I didn't have the slightest idea what I wanted. I only knew that I died of pleasure whenever I was near her.

"I should also say that to be in my mother's house was to be in an inferno of love. Everything was about love: the two women, their lovers, their toilettes, the liquors, perfumes, songs and dances. Even the grotesque and dramatic exits of their lovers had an air of voluptuousness and passion. It was only the arrival of my father and the brutality that followed that was antithetical to love. But we even accepted this as the price to be paid for pleasure. Or as my mother said, 'All good things have their opposites; we even pay for life with death. And that's why life must be lived. Live, my children, according to your desires so that you'll have nothing to regret when Judgment Day arrives.'

"With such a philosophy for a guide, is it any wonder that Kyra and I followed our mother's example?

"My mother's personal fortune was in the hands of her brothers who made their living smuggling Oriental goods. This allowed her to pay for every pleasure her desire dictated. Adored, she changed lovers as often as her dresses. And though she always defended her face, she suffered my father's blows. Afterward, she promptly found a new distraction.

"She even had a certain virtue: when she knew she'd have to reckon for what she had done, and was worried that her husband's rage would also spill over onto us, she kept the door bolted until we'd been able to jump out the back windows. She would then bravely open it, and take all the abuse herself.

"When we returned several hours later, we'd find her stretched out on the sofa, her face covered in little gobs of white bread soaked in red wine—her remedy for lessening the swelling and bruises. She'd sit up, laughing like a madwoman, and with a mirror in her hand she'd display her battered face, saying to us, 'It's not such a big thing, is it? In a couple of days there won't be a trace left of the beating. And then we'll invite the *moussafirs* again. So what if we have to get beaten.'

"We were both disturbed about the blows her body had taken, and were frightened over how her flesh must look.

She'd exclaim, "Oh, my body! No one can see my body!

"And when the bruises had disappeared, the festivities began again, as beautiful as always.

"We never made any sort of meal in the house since my mother's heart was quickened by the smell of roasted onions. She had everything we needed sent in from a neighboring inn—a *locanda.* They furnished soups, meats, cakes, custards. All arrived in silver-plated vessels that my mother supplied. Each Monday morning a laundry lady brought fresh linens for the week and took away what needed washing. Only those people and the old Turk who sold lotions and drugs ever entered the house, with the exception, of course, of the *moussafirs* who could never be sure of leaving the same way they'd entered. The only others who came were my father and older brother, the non-invited *moussafirs,* whose visits we always despised. For around two years my father had not slept with my mother and only came three or four times per month to beat us. Except when he appeared, the house was tranquil.

"Exempt from domestic chores the two women passed their time relaxing: taking baths, doing their toilettes, eating, drinking, smoking hookahs, and receiving their guests. They never forgot their prayers though they never went to church. And the time they spent in service to God was quite short. My mother excused herself, saying, 'God can see quite well that I'm not living contrary to His will: I am she whom He made. I listen quite attentively to the cries and commands of my heart.'

"Kyra objected. 'But Mama, don't you think the devil sometimes mixes himself into it?'

"'No,' she replied. I don't believe in the devil. God is stronger than he is. And we are who we are because God wanted us that way.'

"And certainly, my mother was content to do as God wished her to do, since he hadn't wished her to be miserable.

"First, He wished that my mother and her daughter linger in bed in the morning as long as He wanted. And in bed was the best place to savor rolls with butter and honey and drink coffee. He ordered them next to bathe themselves, anoint their bodies with benzoin tincture, and let the vapor of simmered milk steam their faces. Then to make their hair shine, they were to massage their scalps with almond oil perfumed with musk. To improve the luster of their nails, they painted them with a little brush dipped in a cashew balm. Next, it was time to apply, with the utmost skill, makeup to their eyebrows, eyelashes, lips and cheeks. And when all this was finished, it was time for lunch, smoking and napping until the sun had set. Upon rising, they lit incense, drank syrups, and finally they began the longest part of their day in which they sang and danced until midnight.

"My mother was much richer than my father, and despite the crazy way she spent her fortune, placed in the shady businesses of her brothers, it returned such large sums that each month she was able to invest, always with her brothers, money destined for Kyra and me.

"I don't know much of my mother's story. What I do remember is her telling us frequently that her parents were rich hotel keepers. Her father, a good and pious Turk, was sent at the end of the 18th Century from Stamboul, with a decree from the Ottoman Sublime Port to open a hotel in Ibraïla. His mission was to entertain and lodge all the exalted personages sent by the Sultan to the region. He had three wives, two Greeks and a Romanian. The latter was my mother's mother; the others, mothers of three boys, one of whom went mad and hanged himself. But my mother, as well as her two brothers from the other bed, only got on in my grandfather's house when they were engaged in mischief. It seems that nothing more interesting took place in that house than squirreling away money and praying to God in three different languages.

"The two boys threw themselves into smuggling and my mother, also quite young, was prepared to follow them, but the good Turk decided to marry her off quickly to a hard and heartless man, my father, who became infatuated with her probably, as my mother said, at a moment when God was blowing His nose. My grandfather gave my father a lot of gold and bequeathed a large part of his fortune to her, with the right to administer it as she wanted so long as she remained married. In compliance with the Turk's demand, she stayed with the man she detested fearing she'd be disinherited if she didn't. After several years of awful fidelity, she gained her father's confidence, and when he died she managed to grab her fortune and place it into the hands of her brothers, who adored her.

"That was when the good life began, the life of parties, pleasures and crazy love affairs that I saw with my own eyes and which my father, despite his constant brutality, could not suppress. My mother would have willingly made him a present of her dowry if it would have given her freedom, but he was set on taking revenge on her for dishonoring him. The day of their separation he took all that belonged to him, and said to my mother, in front of Kyra and me, 'These two snakes I leave to you. They are not my children; they are like their mother.'

"'Would you have them be like their father?' she replied. 'You're a shriveled man, a corpse who interferes with the living being able to live. I am even astonished that one as dead as you could have brought into life this other dry twig who is certainly your child but not mine.'

"My poor mother was right to say that that corpse interfered with our lives. It got worse and worse. My father knew that my mother loved her face more than life, and so he made sure he struck her there. This last time, it took eight or ten days for my suffering mother to recover from the mass of welts and bruises. During the time she healed there was no question of her enjoying herself nor of receiving the *moussafirs*. This threw her into a depression. She didn't hug or kiss us as before; and for the first time I saw her cry in total despair.

"But this despair gave way to furious revenge against my father. Her rage was so great that it served to increase the tyrant's fury. And her success in infuriating him would ultimately prove fatal.

"One evening the house was wall to wall with at least seven *moussafirs*. My mother had hung four sconces on the walls, and overhead was the grand chandelier. I counted the candles: there were twenty-eight. The illumination was blinding. That same day she had called in a locksmith to fix a large bolt to the massive courtyard door that up until then closed only with a lock and key. With the door thus secured, she was filled with an overwhelming joy that I had never seen before. I now think that that she knew that the happy life was coming to an end, and she wanted to live as fully and intensely as she could.

"Of the seven guests, three were Greek musicians who were quite well known at the time for entertaining at parties. At the beginning of the ball my mother gave each one a little leather purse containing ten gold ducats of twelve francs wrapped in an embroidered silk handkerchief.

"'My gallant *palicarias*—gentlemen! You have in your purses five times more than what you should receive for playing all night! I don't give you this only because I'm generous. In this house one pays dearly for joy, and it might be that you will be obliged to leave through the windows: do you have good legs?'

"And she opened the windows overlooking the ravine. The *palicarias* leaned out and surveyed the terrain, all the while weighing the weight of the gold as they made the purses dance in their hands. Finally, they accepted the deal with a courteous cry of '*Eyvallah!*'

"The game, the songs, the dance began.

"They played their three instruments—clarinet, fife and guitar—quite skillfully. Kyra and mother lay stretched out next to one another on the sofa listening in rapture to the plaintive, then lively, Romanian *doinas*, languid Turkish *maniebs*, and Greek pastorals, all accompanied by the singing and clapping of the four *moussafirs*.

"After each game and song mother served liquors, coffee and hookahs. Two large and sumptuous plates of Turkish cakes—*kadayifs* and *sarailes*—were passed in front of the eyes of the gourmands.

"Since I was not on watch that evening I danced with my sister and my mother, by myself, and with both of them together, until I was almost dizzy. The great passion of my short childhood in that house was to get Kyra to hold me in a wild embrace. The belly dance I performed alone on that last night of festivities was so rich in it movements that the musicians, who were connoisseurs, effusively complemented and kissed me. Kyra was beside herself, and my mother exclaimed:

"'Oh yes! He is definitely my son; there not a doubt about it.'

"During a break, while all the men were squatting Turkish style on the rug, smoking their hookahs with gusto, Kyra asked what had happened to one of her most assiduous admirers.

"'His ankle got twisted from tumbling down the hill on the night of the last party,' said one of the party goers. And in the general hilarity, he explained how the good man was at that moment lying in bed, raging about it to his masseur. This caused the guitarist some grief, as he was fat and less than agile. He went to the window to measure the distance with his eye. A *moussafir* tried to reassure him:

"'It's not so high. Two meters at the most. But you must not jump out too far. Instead just slide down gently and you'll find yourself gliding down the hill. At the bottom you'll find your fez and guitar.'

"Everyone laughed, and the dancing began again."

"That event happened in the month of June, a little before the harvest.

"On the side of the courtyard the windows were draped in heavy curtains, while those that opened onto the Danube were only sheers. And we were all tired when, on that morning, the dawn spread its bleached golden rays across the window panes. We danced. The air was filled with hookah smoke so thick the incense had little effect.

"My mother went to the window, opened it, and breathed in deeply the fresh morning air. Kyra and I stood at her side watching the marshes and willow grove gradually becoming clear in the morning light. She then turned to the revelers, 'Well, my friends, the party's over. We're going to bed'

"At that very moment the sound of a body falling heavily into the courtyard startled us, and not long after, we heard the bolt being slid open and the groans of the door opening. My mother cried out, 'Save yourselves! They've scaled the wall!'

"And while my father and his son pounded on the door, the guests jumped out the two back windows, forgetting any precautions, as if outside woolen mattresses were in place to receive them. The musicians were the first to flee; the others followed right on their behinds, heedless of their warning not to jump out too far. In just a few seconds the house was emptied of guests as the *moussafirs*, one after another, rolled down the sandy slope. There wasn't time even to think about removing the traces of the party.

"And so, bravely, my mother went to open up. She was immediately grabbed by her hair and thrown to the floor; the brother did the same to Kyra; and I, in a panic at seeing my sister so cruelly kicked, grabbed a hookah and smashed my brother's head with it. He let go of Kyra, rubbed his bleeding head, and lit into me. He was nearly twenty and very strong. I was beaten until blood ran from my nose and mouth.

"While I was getting thrashed my mother was getting the life beaten out of her. Her clothes were in tatters, her body almost naked, and though she was unconscious, my father continued to pound her. When my brother went to wash his bloody head Kyra ran to the dressing table, returning with a stiletto in her hand. But we were both frozen in terror by the horror that met out eyes: my father had picked up a wooden-heeled sandal, lost in the flight of one of the *moussafirs*, and was bringing it down with all his might on my mother's face. Her face, bathed in blood, was reduced to a mass of wounds.

"Kyra ran toward the barbarian to plunge the knife into his back but staggered, then fell in a faint to the floor. My father picked her up and threw her into a wardrobe that he quickly bolted. I was left under the guard of my brother who was bandaging his head with a large handkerchief. My father then picked up my mother and went into the courtyard where a few minutes later I heard the heavy trap door to the cellar bang shut, enclosing my mother as if in a tomb. When he reentered he came at me with his fists clenched, and I believed that my final hour had come. But he didn't touch me. Instead, he said, 'So that's what you were up to, huh? You break open your brother's head, and that whore of a sister of yours wanted to kill me. Well now, all of you are done for.'

"They extinguished the candles and marched me out of the room. As we passed through the courtyard I glanced at the trap door. Two heavy chains, padlocked with rings, made any escape impossible. I began to cry at the idea of my poor mother, barely alive, bleeding and bruised, interred in that horrible tomb, while Kyra, shut up in the wardrobe, was suffocating in despair.

"Outside, the day had commenced. Some Turkish charcoal makers, with bundles on their backs and pointed canes under their arms, were going toward the port to work. And I? Where was I going?

"We arrived at my father's house and I was quickly put to turning the grindstone on which the apprentices sharpened their axes, scissors and dulled gouges. Scattered around me here and there were trunks of oak and linden and poplar, as well as pieces of wagons: wheels, hubs, spokes, carriage poles and rims. Everything was covered with heaps of wood shavings.

"They didn't give me anything to eat until noon. And since I wasn't used to working I became terribly weak. My brother whipped me, and the old servant brought me nothing but bread, olives and water.

"It was all made worse because I was being watched by everyone, and there wasn't any way I could escape. In the afternoon I turned the grindstone again, and when I couldn't manage it any longer, my brother came over and kicked me in the legs. He and his father wore leather aprons as did all the workers, and whether they were working or coming and going, they were always grave and morose with their brows knit. It was a cheerless atmosphere. The only sounds were the clanging of tools and the occasional sharp, brief grunts of orders.

"That night I was shut up in a room with barred windows. There, on a straw mat thrown on the floor and without light I spent the night crying and thinking about my dear mother and sister, who had been treated far worse than I.

"The next day was identical to the first. I asked myself over and over, my anxiety mounting, if my barbarous father was going to leave my mother and sister, so bruised and beaten, to die. That night, I decided to stop crying and concentrate on escaping.

"I had noticed in the courtyard that there were ladders of all lengths, and in my cell there were heaps of defective spokes. These were, in effect, my keys to freedom. The servant brought my dinner—bread and cheese—and said to me menacingly, 'It's not as comfortable here as it is at home, is it? Life, you see, is not just about pleasure; there's also pain, right?'

"She shut the door, and I fell asleep. When I awakened, it was already night. I lay awake crying, remembering the bloodied face of my mother. Then, when the cocks began to crow I saw the sun beginning to rise. The house was plunged in sleep. Rapidly, I opened the window, and with a spoke, I carefully spread the thinnest of the bars. In the courtyard, an ax was planted in a tree trunk. I pulled it out, grabbed a little ladder and tucked it under my arm, and scaled the wall using another ladder. Once on the other side I ran as fast as my legs could carry me to the road that flanked the port.

"It was barely daylight when I arrived at the base of the hill that led to our house, gripped in the sleep of despair. And for the first time I climbed up that slope that before I had only descended in a hurry.

"Arriving at the top I put up the ladder, and with my heart beating, I broke out the window. It shattered into shards. Then after a few moments, racked with emotion, I heard Kyra's sweet voice crying out from the wardrobe, 'Is that you, Dragomir?'

"Upon hearing my name called by my dearest sister, imprisoned in the wardrobe, I was overcome and cried out, 'Yes, it's me. I've come to get you out.'

"I crawled through the opening I'd made in the window and jumped inside. In a flash, I unbolted the lock. Kyra was ghostly pale, her face swelled from weeping. She threw her arms around my neck, beseeching me to tell her where mother was.

"'She's locked in the cellar; we've got to get her out of there, and get ourselves out of here.'

"The door to the house was locked with a key, so I opened a window and jumped down into the courtyard. With the blows of my hatchet, I broke the rings holding the lock on the trap door and bounded down the stairs followed by Kyra. The odor of mold, sauerkraut and rotted vegetables wafted into my nostrils, for nobody had been down in the cellar for two or three years. Some tortoises moved about slowly, and their eggs, a little larger than birds' eggs, were visible along the length of the wall. In this miserable place my mother had been confined for more than forty-eight hours.

"When we discovered her she was standing, her head swaddled in bandages made from her ripped clothes that hung on her in tatters. We helped her up the slimy stairs. Once outside the spectacle of what remained of my beautiful mother caused us to fall to our knees as if in front of a martyr. One eye was hidden under a bandage, but judging from the rest of her swollen and bruised face, we knew what it must be like. Her nose was broken, her lips ripped, her neck and breasts covered with dried blood. Her hands, too, were bloody, and one finger was broken.

"She asked us to rise, and said in a hollow voice, 'We must get out of here. And take with you a little something to eat.'

"We went back into the house, where quickly they washed up and dressed themselves in dull clothes. My mother grabbed her jewelry box, and we exited through the window, throwing the ladder back into the house. We then carefully went down the hill that so many *moussafirs* had descended in order to save themselves. Fate decreed that the mistress of the house would be the last one ever to exit it like that.

"An hour later we got the road to Cazassou, completely surrounded by wheat fields. In front of two little hills that were dubbed *tabiës*, or forts, my mother stopped. There, sitting on the grass between the two *tabiës* that hid us from the road, my mother spoke to us in a voice that revealed her anxiety, 'My children, I expected a lot of meanness on the part of your father but I didn't expect to be disfigured without being killed by the same blow. You should know that my left eye is nearly de-tached from its socket. For me this is worse than death. I was made by the Lord for the pleasures of the flesh, just as he made the mole to live under-ground without light. And just as that creature has everything it needs to live in the earth, I was lacking nothing to enjoy my life of pleasure. I made a vow to kill myself if I were forced by men to knuckle under and live a life other than what my body and soul dictated. Today, I am thinking about that vow. I'm going to leave you. I'm going to journey a long way from our house. And if it happens that my eye can be saved, and all traces of ugliness disappear, I will go on living, and you will see me again. But if my eye is lost, you will never see me again. And, Kyra, listen to what I have to say to you. If you Kyra, as I believe, do not feel the need to live a life of virtue, then don't. Don't be virtuous if it means you are constrained and shriveled inside. Don't mock God. Strive to be the best in how He made you. Seek pleasure, even debauchery, but don't let debauchery harden your heart. It's better like that. And you, Dragomir, if you cannot be a virtuous man be like your sister and your mother, be a thief even, but a thief who has a heart, for a man without a heart, my children, is a corpse that keeps the living from living their lives. Your father...'

"'Now stay here until the sun is three lance lengths above the horizon. If it rains, or there is thunder do not go looking for a tree under which to take shelter but instead, hide in that hole that you can see in the hollow of the hill. A little after vespers two men on horseback will come here to get you and protect you. They are my brothers, two men of great heart and true deeds. I cannot lead you to them, though that is where I am going now, for you are still children and could unwittingly betray them. And if for some reason they don't come when I said, go back to the city and ask, in my name, for a room at the *locanda* from which we used to get our food. But do not leave your room until my brothers come to fetch you. I also have one more thing to say: our bodies are subject to frightful ailments. By the grace of God neither you nor I have been afflicted, but a great many have not escaped. Think of them in your happy moments and give every year part of your money to those who care for them. I will leave plenty of money for you with my brothers.'

"After these words, she got out her jewelry box and removed two rings, tied them in a silk handkerchief, and hid them in Kyra's bodice. We kissed one another for a very long time. And then she left, entirely covered with her hooded cape.

"After she had taken thirty steps, she turned toward us and pressed her hands against her lips. Then raising her arms above her head she pointed with an index finger toward the canopy of heaven, then turned her back and disappeared.

"'What does that mean?' I asked Kyra.

"'That means, my dear brother, that we will see her again in heaven.'

"I never saw my mother again.

"Left alone we forgot that we were famished, and we wept, holding one another until exhaustion and the heat of the sun lulled us into a much needed sleep. On awakening we had the impression that we were no longer part of this world, that something catastrophic had come to pass. We didn't know whether we were in the midst of a nightmare, or whether our life up until that moment had been a dream. A light stifling breeze carried the smell of cabbage which filled the field in front of us. Butterflies, dragonflies and wasps whirled around us in wild joyful arcs.

"The hour of vespers had arrived. The sun, sinking toward the horizon, lost its brilliance. Uneasily we waited, and began scrutinizing the lonely road where our mother had disappeared. We had no sooner climbed up one of the hills to get a better view when we saw a cloud of dust rising a good distance down the road. Within a few minutes, two horsemen appeared, riding at a gallop, with a train of dust trailing behind them. I was afraid and crouched down, for I feared being trampled by the horses' hooves whose rhythmical pounding filled my ears. Unlike me, Kyra stood tall on the crest of the hill, her light skirt blowing in the breeze, waving her handkerchief and crying out with joy at the arrival of the two horsemen. The two men held back on the reins of their stallions and entered the field between the two hills, then loosened the bits of the horses so that their steeds could munch some grass.

"Kyra rapidly ran down the slope, undoing her headband so that her beautiful golden hair could fall to her shoulders. She threw herself at the feet of our unknown uncles who were now in front of us, looming as tall and large as two oak trees. The two colossal men seemed to be between forty and fifty years old, one a little younger than the other. They wore turbans on their shaved heads and sported beards and mustaches that nearly hid their mouths. Their large eyes were penetrating and hard but clear and frank, and their hairy hands looked like bear paws. They were as black as devils in their *ghébas* or peasant robes that enveloped them from their necks to their knees.

"They stayed still for a moment, looking at us. I stood there, thinking that I was in the presence of apparitions. Kyra remained prostrate at their feet. They then removed their robes and I saw that they were dressed like Turks: vests, flowing trousers, wide red woolen belts. But what most cap-

tivated and terrified me was that they were armed to the teeth, like real
antartes—Greek robbers. They had short barreled arquebuses draped over
their shoulders and pistols and knives stuck in their belts.

"In the midst of my observations, Kyra let her stifled rage resound
like a clap of thunder. She pleaded with the two strong men to destroy a
family, and then exhausted, fell to the ground, a victim of her own venge-
ful passion.

"The older of the men picked Kyra up and looked in her eyes, his
hands on her shoulders. What I took at first for a grimace emerging from
the forest of whiskers that covered his face, I quickly realized was a smile.
The smile was even more defined in his eyes. In Romanian he said, in a
low metallic voice, 'Little girl! Tell me, which language—Turkish, Greek
or Romanian—do you speak the best.'

"'Romanian, oh, *cruce de voinic*—oh mighty one—' she answered
courageously, fixing her eyes directly on him.

"'And your name?'

"'Kyra.'

"'Ah, good, Kyra. I'll kiss you like an uncle, but he who bites your
cherry-red lips will be a happy man.'

"He kissed her, as did his brother.

"'And you, my good Dragomir, why are you looking so frightened?'
he asked, as he kissed me. He laid his arquebus on his robe. 'Are you
afraid of our beards?'

"He lay down on the grass and pulled me toward him. I still didn't
dare to speak. "'Tell me, Dragomir, are you a little afraid?'

"'Yes,' I responded, timidly.

"'Why are you afraid?'

"'You have so many weapons.'

"He began to laugh loudly. 'Ha, ha, ha, my good Dragomir! One can
never have too many weapons when you have swept aside God's laws and
those of all his creatures. But you can't understand that at your age,'

"Kyra rose to her knees, put her hands together as if to pray, and cried
out, 'I understand it!'

"'And what do you understand, Kyra Kyralina, my young rosebud?'

"'I understand that some men are evil, and that you will punish them!'

"'Bravo, Kyralina!' he shouted, clapping his hand together. 'Does your young heart feed on revenge?'

"'A holy and just revenge!' And after saying this she lifted the heavy arquebus that was lying on the robe, kissed it, and cried out, 'By tonight you must shoot this into the chest of my father! And your brother will deliver the same justice to my older brother. Do this, please, I beg of you, in the name of our mother who has left us. If you take revenge for us, two orphans, I will be your slave. You can take me with you!'

"Our uncle took the weapon in his hands and spoke somberly, 'Kyra, God erred when he made you a woman. When you spoke of vengeance, I thought that you wanted me to chastise one of your lovers who had kissed you against your will. But you speak of things about which we have already been thinking. You only added fuel to our fire.' And after a short pause, he continued, 'Tell me, child of hell, won't you be deathly afraid when you see tonight your father's head bursting into pieces?'

"Kyra's eyes flashed, as red as fire, and she said, 'I will wash my hands in his blood and bathe my face with it!'

"Our uncle winced and turned to look at the last rays of the setting sun, as if he had his ear cocked to listen for the distant sound of a plaintive shepherd's flute. Then, he began speaking in Greek with his brother, clipping his words, to make them even more difficult to understand.

"As the night fell upon the two *tabiës* plunging them in darkness, the horses munched the grass and snorted, as docile as sheep.

"No one spoke. The cool freshness of the air made Kyra shiver. Our uncles wrapped their robes around us, continuing their conversation in low, deep voices. We stayed this way until darkness enshrouded us. The two men then rose. The older one said to my sister, 'Very well, Kyra Kyralina, my sweet-breathed snake, daughter of a libertine. It will be as you wish! Your desire to bathe in blood will be realized. We will attempt it this evening. And to pull it off you and your brother will serve as our bait.'

"Kyra bent on her knee and kissed his hand. I did likewise, kissing the hand of my other uncle who asked, 'Dragomir, do you too want revenge?'

"'I hate my father and my brother.'

"The older one mounted his horse and lifted up Kyra, sitting her in front of him while the younger one hoisted me into the saddle and tied me to him with a strap. The horses sauntered out of the field but once on the road the older one spurred his horse into a gallop, and we followed apace, twenty steps behind.

"In the time it takes to smoke a cigarette we had arrived at the edge of the city. We turned left onto a road that led in a straight line to the Danube. Our pace was so fast that I thought for a few minutes that I was riding with the devil. In the beautiful moonlight that turned the road silver, Kyra's hair escaping from her hood blew in the wind like golden threads unwinding from a spinning wheel.

"A little afterward we began to descend a hill. When the bank of the sparkling river came into sight the horses slowed their breakneck speed, and then came to a quick halt at the edge of a willow grove. We found ourselves at Katagatz, an hour on foot away from the harbor and our house. Without dismounting our two uncles drew alongside one another and exchanged a few words, which I could not understand at all. The older one then put two fingers to his lips and gave a long and piercing whistle, followed, after a pause, by two short notes.

"In a moment or two an old Turk with a long white beard scuffled out of the grove. On nearing us he uttered an *Asalaam 'Alaykum,* and bowed respectfully, his arms crossed across his chest.

"My uncles spoke to him in Turkish. 'Good evening, Ibrahim.'

"He took the horses by their bridles, and we followed behind. On the other side of the grove, facing the Danube, was his house, that was flooded frequently by the rising river. He was a crayfish fisherman and also grew a few watermelons. You can easily guess what his third job was. He tied up the horses under a reed arbor and entered his shack, followed by our older uncle. Our uncle reemerged in a couple of minutes, took Kyra in his arms, and with giant strides carried her away quickly. The younger uncle did the same with me as if we were two infants. The two men made their way along the bank toward the harbor. Dry branches cracked under their feet.

"Once we'd arrived at the bottom of the hill, we began to crawl. The house was plunged in darkness, but we noted that the window I had broken had been covered and nailed shut with planks. My uncles listened for even the slightest sound. Hearing nothing, they smashed the boards with their gun stocks and we entered. The older one said, 'We'll go through the courtyard and hide in the cellar. If we have to, we can stay there until morning. Close the window, light six or eight candles, eat something, and then, without undressing, lie down on the sofa. Do you understand? On the sofa and without putting out the candles! If they come and begin questioning you, tell them whatever you want. But leave the drapes open on the windows facing the courtyard. That's of utmost importance. And don't forget to stay on the sofa.

"Ah! How long the hours were that night. If I live to be a thousand, I would still remember every terrible second of that ordeal.

"I hated my pitiless father, as well as that offspring of a creature who resembled him. I wanted nothing more than that the devil would carry off both of them. To want someone to vanish is a natural outcome of hate, but to participate in killing someone takes something more than hate. But what? What did it take? I didn't know. I wanted to say that it took cruelty, but Kyra wasn't cruel. Of that I was sure.

"It's a sad thing to be a man and not understand life any better than does a dumb beast. Why does pity live alongside hate? And why does one love someone? And why does one kill someone? Why do we succumb to feelings that wrong others and ourselves?

"Alone, after we had lighted the candles, the first thing I did was to look into Kyra's eyes. Her desire for murder was as pronounced as had been her desire for a party. She was in ecstasy. She put on a low-necked dress and made herself up as if she were going to host the *moussafirs.* And she never stopped singing for a moment. Her left cheek was violet and swollen as large as a walnut.

"'Kiss that hard!' she told me. Tonight, the blast of an arquebus will make it vanish.'

"'Kyra,' I said, as I kissed her bruise, 'wouldn't it be better to call our uncles and go away with them?'

"'No!' she cried emphatically. 'The one who murdered our mother must be punished. Then we can leave.'

"'But it's going to be frightful to see!'

"'It's going to be beautiful!' she answered, taking me in her arms and kissing me.

"The minutes went by slowly and terribly, as if in a nightmare. I held on to the hope that my father and brother might not come that evening, nor on the nights that followed, and that my uncles would abandon their project. For all I knew the *ursilele,* the three fairies who preside over births, might have decided to overrule our desire. But who knows if what Kyra so desired wasn't also what they wanted.

"Kyra ran back and forth between the mirror, where she kept looking at herself, and the windows that opened on to the courtyard. She danced with her veil, kissed her tresses, and now and then would throw herself on the cushions, laughing strangely. Then, suddenly she became very pensive, and went into the adjoining room. She returned with a little dagger.

"'Do you see this?' she whispered. "'If you betray the presence of our uncles I'll stab this into my heart. And you'll be all alone. I swear by mother I'll do it!'

"I was stunned. Such an idea had never occurred to me. 'Put it back in its place, Kyra,' I begged. 'I swear, also by my mother, that I won't say a word.'

"But she sequestered the dagger in her dress.

"She had just hidden the dagger when the hinges on the door began to groan plaintively. The sound resonated in my heart like a scream of death. Kyra shivered and her eyes flashed. She threw herself down next to me on the sofa and whispered into my ear, 'Don't look at the windows into the courtyard! Never! Never!'

"The key turned in the lock; and frozen, glued to Kyra, I saw my father followed by my brother. He was scowling and his fists were clenched.

"'Who broke through the window there, you or your mother?' he asked, pointing to the broken planks.

"Two shots, almost simultaneously, sent shards of glass from the courtyard windows raining down on the room, filling the air with thick smoke that smelled of burnt rags and powder. Tight in Kyra's arms, I couldn't see anything in those terrible seconds except for my brother falling backwards to the floor and my father leaping through the back window. I closed my eyes, suffocating. When I forced myself to reopen them I saw my brother lying on the floor, his head burst open like a watermelon that had been smashed against a wall. My uncles were at the window, firing their pistols four times at my father who was running down the hill.

"Kyra freed herself from me and leaped into the middle of the room, crying, 'You missed! You missed! You only shot off his left ear!'

"My uncles' only response was to blow out the candles, and the younger one went out into the courtyard while the older one took us into the vestibule. He asked us to sit down on a divan, and in the pitch blackness said, 'I kiss you, Kyralina and Dragomir, for perhaps the last time. Your father is the third man I've missed, and if I am to put faith in my *ursita*, my destiny, death will come for me at the hand of my third enemy which my arquebus failed to kill under the moonlight. To be sure, I'll do all I can to save my skin, but you can't outwit destiny. Now listen! The owner of the hotel who supplied you with meals will arrive in a moment or two to get you. At his place you will be given two rooms and all the necessities. Tomorrow, he will come back here to bring you your personal things. You must never put a foot in this house again. Never!'

"'Aren't you going to take us with you?' asked Kyra, her voice trembling.

"'No, that I cannot do. Our life is hard and you have been raised in comfort.'

"'But our father will kill us.'

"'He won't kill you. It won't be long before we'll get another chance at him, and this time he won't escape. One way or the other, he's finished. There are two of us, and he's only one. Live according to your wishes and act as if you have never known us. You won't see us again until that dog is dead. If from time to time you need to know if we're still with the living, go to the innkeeper and say my first name: Cosma. He'll tell you what you need to know. But an even better source of information is Ibrahim, the crayfish catcher at Katagatz. If ever, under your window, you hear him crying out 'Fresh Crayfish, Crayfish!' go down and follow him out of the city. He will have some news of us. Finally, if the authorities should ever question you about what happened here tonight, tell them everything you saw but not what you think about it, and don't think about anything!'

"We heard footsteps in the courtyard and soon the innkeeper entered. My uncle kissed us and disappeared, and we left shortly afterward.

"The hotel was about fifty feet from our house and similar to ours. But what a difference in comfort between our rooms and the simple ones we were given, even though they were the best in the house. The basic furniture was beat up, and the carpet worn. Fortunately, the rooms were side-by-side and connected, and the windows looked out over the Danube. Still, we cried until no more tears could be shed.

"In front of the flickering flame of a single candle, Kyra undressed, throwing her clothes on the bed. She was feeling deeply how insane was revenge and cried even more strongly than I.

"Scared at finding myself alone in my room, my eyes filled with the horrors of all that had passed, I grabbed my covers and went to sleep on the sofa in Kyra's room. Exhausted by three days of torture, I drifted quickly to sleep, leaving the candles lit and Kyra sobbing.

"The next morning I felt somewhat better, and as the first rays of the sun lighted my room, it even looked pretty. But the idea that my father might return still made me fearful. I woke up Kyra, who was still sleeping, and proposed that we escape. She agreed. Her eyes red, her face swollen, she sat hunched over on the bed. I thought that maybe she was feeling remorseful.

"'No,' she said. 'I'm just upset that our father managed to escape. If he had been sent on at the same moment as his son, we would be at this moment in our house. This ugly place disgusts me.'

"She threw a disdainful glance around the room, and we decided to go out. In the doorway, in the freshness of the morning, the innkeeper was smoking his hookah. He rose and bowed to us.

"'May I ask why you are going out so early?' he asked respectfully, in Turkish.

"'Abou-Hassan, we are afraid of the police and of our father,' stated Kyra, also in Turkish.

"'I can vouch for your safety, miss, as long as you stay quietly in my inn.' He turned his head to look behind him, then said in a low voice, 'You are here for that reason.'

"I didn't know anything about who this man was nor what his business had been with my mother's family. But I did know for sure that no one had come here to cause us trouble, nor had my father shown up. But since we didn't trust anyone, we made ourselves scarce around the hotel. Thus began our bittersweet life, in which we passed a month wandering in sunlight and in shade.

"This freedom was a new thing for us, a delightful life we'd never known. We were like two birds who had flown their cages and were trying out their wings, soaring into light.

"The inn had a back entrance that while grimy, was very useful to us as it allowed us to go in and out without being seen. The little door opened onto a rudimentary stairway, just below our windows, that led to the bank alongside the port. Once we had become accustomed to our crude new entrance and exit, we joked that it was better than what we had at the house, for the hill below our mother's didn't have a stairway.

"After we had had an early breakfast, we went out until around noon. We took lunch in our rooms. In the afternoon, we returned to the outside world. As the harvest was over, Kyra took great pleasure in gathering together wheat kernels and making them into bundles to give to the poor old women gleaners who were bent over from working so long in the fields. We also ran through the fallow fields where thousands of ewes roamed this way and that, leaving behind them the dirt covered with dung and tufts of wool that got caught on thistles. Some old women went from thistle to thistle gathering the little tufts and balling them up to make roving. We did likewise, and turned over to them our happily gathered tuft balls.

"Once we wandered further, all the way to the *tabiés* where our mother had left us. There we discovered the food bundle we had left behind on the night we had been rescued by our uncles. Stray dogs had ripped the package open and eaten the food; only a few rags were left.

"This discovery made us begin crying again. The memory of the disastrous events that had befallen us seemed even sadder as we had been having some good days, and were even beginning to forget our misery. These moments of pain alternated seamlessly with other hours of happiness that swelled our breasts with joy. Brought up 'in comfort' as my Uncle Cosma had said, we had only known the pleasures of our mother's house: the dances, the songs, the meals, the flirting. That, of course, was wonderful. But now we were discovering that there was an outside world, and that this world was even better: rich and light-filled, perfumed with the wild scents of nature. We had never known what it was like to chase a butterfly, to catch a green grasshopper, to trap giant bumblebees, to listen to birds serenade their vast empire, to hear the crickets, invisible at nightfall, mix their songs with the distant flute of a shepherd, and to see honey bees dart in and out of flowers, their legs dripping with pollen. And even more, we had never had any idea of how totally splendid it was to be caressed by the breeze blowing off the fields of summer.

"In getting to know these pleasures we forgot the taste of cakes; forgotten, too, was the lure of the dance, the smell of hookah smoke, and the aroma of incense. Forgotten, too, were our disfigured mother and our desire for vengeance. Kyra tanned within a few days from being outside, and there was never a more beautiful woman who ran through a field, her eyes dewy with love, her hair streaming behind her like a golden banner, her skirt raised well above her knees, her voluptuous breasts offered to the

Sun God.

"During that time a story sprang up around the neighborhood. According to the rumor it was my mother's lovers who had killed my brother and shot off my father's left ear. People even went so far as to give the names of the two *moussafirs* who, by a strange coincidence had embarked for Stamboul the very night of the tragedy. This led us to understand that our father was keeping secret the murder of his son and had not filed a complaint with the police.

"We began to relax because of this news, and returned to our rambles with much less worry. But Kyra began to tire of our games in the woods and fields. What had happened, you see, was that her *moussafirs* had begun to mingle around our new quarters. Crouched beneath our windows overlooking the port where there were few passersby, they took up serenading us every night. Ridiculously perched on the steps of the stairway they played incessantly. More and more came every night. It made us laugh to see these fools assembled up and down the hill, braying and cacophonously playing their instruments. Though thick as thieves they squabbled with each other and from time to time were pushed by their exuberance to roll down the slope.

"The amused Kyra and me, and we enjoyed staring down at them from our windows. They were always trying to persuade us to join them or let them join us. Abou-Hassan would have none of it, and would pour buckets of cold water over their heads. But love is stronger than water, and they continued on with their antics. To incite them even further, Kyra began to make herself up again and play the temptress. This left me alone to wander about in the mornings. I happily did this, but never went too far from the inn. The Danube attracted me like an irresistible force. I was eleven-years-old but had never known the pleasure of gliding along the river on one of the boats on which the rowers languorously sang as they made their way downstream.

"At that time the port didn't have a dock and one could go ten or twenty feet into the water and it would only be chest-high. To reach a boat it was necessary to go out onto little wooden piers that linked to bigger bridges. The big yachts, anchored farther out, rubbed their bows against the pontoons that supported the large bridges that were sturdily made out of blocks and boards. A squad of Turk, Armenian and Romanian stevedores, cargo on their backs, steadily went back and forth across the bridges that sagged under their weight.

"I began by watching this world from a distance, but after a while I began to mix in with kids from the four or five countries who lived in the town, enjoying their games. Above all I liked seeing them bathe, as naked as little brown devils. I wanted to go in the river with them, but I was afraid of their rough horsing. They were always having water fights, holding each other's heads under the water until they were struggling to breathe. And one day they almost drowned a little boy, blonde like me, whom they had dragged to the river.

"After that I moved on, contenting myself with watching the boatmen who smoked or sang as they guided the boats along the river. One day I asked one of them, a Turk, to take me out for a bit on the water. He told me that to go for a ride on his boat, I'd have to pay him. I didn't know that you were supposed to carry money and pay for things since I'd never had to do it. He thought I was stupid and explained to me that the way he earned his living was by transporting people from place to place on the river. While speaking to me he looked from time to time behind me, winking, and finally after observing closely how I was dressed, exclaimed, 'Ah these rich children! They don't know that you have to have money to live!

"I turned and saw an old Turk, beautifully and richly attired, leaning on a knotted wooden cane who, though a short distance away, was listening to our conversation. He called me over by wiggling his finger and said, 'Are you Turkish? You speak the language well.'

"'No,' I said, 'I'm Romanian.'

"He questioned me for a long time. I answered some of what he asked but did not respond to his polite but personal questions. But I was nonetheless drawn to him. Why, oh why at that moment couldn't I have been more prescient?

"I had in front of me that despicable being that shattered both my life and that of Kyra: Nazim Effendi. Like many others at that time he was a yacht owner and procurer of flesh for harems. It was not obvious at first that he was such a monster. He seemed to me courteous, serious, calm and sober. As he took his leave to board his carpeted and cushioned boat, he said off-handedly, 'If by chance, you'd like to go for a sail, alone or with your sister, I'd be happy to oblige.'

"He called over his Arab sailor, gave him a quick command, and off they went onto the river. I was thrilled by his offer and regretted not taking him up on it then and there, for I feared I might not have another opportunity.

"I ran as fast as my legs could carry me to the inn, and as I hurried up the stairway I blew kisses at Kyra who standing at the window.

"'You're not very nice,' she told me, 'to go off and enjoy yourself while leaving me alone in this boring place.'

"'Tomorrow you'll get to enjoy yourself like a princess on the river on a bey's boat,' I cried, throwing my arms around her.

"I then breathlessly recounted the marvelous opportunity presented to me. Oh, why wasn't she savvier than I, more experienced? She devoured my words, and her head began swimming as much as mine, so much so that she lay awake all night in expectation of sailing on the Danube on a luxurious boat.

"The next morning she spent hours getting herself ready and getting me ready. Around mid-day we went down to the edge of the river. The Arab with the little launch was there, but the Turk was not. Audaciously, Kyra asked him, 'Are you still in charge of taking us on the river?'

"'Yes,' he said, as he rose.

"Kyra ran along the pier and jumped onto the open boat as agile as a dog. Then, as I followed I heard behind me a boatman say something that I would recall again and again, 'What nice prey.'

"I repeated these words to Kyra and asked what they meant.

"'They're just stupid words!' she said dismissively.

"A light breeze was blowing, just enough to billow the sail, and for the first time we took in the delight of gliding smoothly along the water. Where the river widened, we headed toward midstream, but as we did little waves began to rock the boat. Kyra was afraid, and cried out, 'Don't go so far out into the middle of the river. Stay close to the port.'

"The Arab turned the rudder and we glided back nearer the shore. The boat passed slowly by our house that sat sadly deserted on the crest above the river. Next to it was the inn with our windows open. Next came the hubbub of the port with its army of stevedores, its sailboats, barges and pontoons. We steered toward the end of the harbor where a lonely little pier jutted out into river. And standing on the other side was the Turk, waiting for us. He came out onto the pier, greeted Kyra with a long low bow, and helped her onto the shore. She was quite flattered. The man moved gracefully, and his manners were impeccably elegant. He was quite the contrast to the hurly-burly *moussafirs*.

"Pity the poor human heart that gives itself over heedlessly to life's joys! How blind we were! How was it that we were so dazed we did not pay more attention nor suspect anything about the Turk's prompt appearance at our arrival, nor notice his calculated departure?

"And his cunning was even more evident when Kyra, seduced by his calm manner, his reserve and his white beard, asked without thinking whether we could visit his yacht. It was, of course, what he wanted; and now certain that he had his prey firmly in his clutches, he responded, 'Not at this moment, my charming young lady. My boat is anchored on the other bank of the river where the Macin feeds into the Danube. It is at this moment being loaded, and since you're not used to the waves, you might become seasick. But I will satisfy your curiosity soon. In the meanwhile my launch is at your service, and I would be honored to see you use it.'

"On saying this, he uttered an *Asalaam 'Alaykum* and bowed deeply, ruffling his silk garments, then put his hands to his forehead, to his lips and to his chest, and boarded his launch.

"This new pleasure made us forget our mother, father, uncles, *moussafirs* and even God, Himself. Our bodies and souls were firmly in our distinguished gentleman's grasp. For three days we availed ourselves of his offer of sailing on the Danube. We went farther and farther out until one day, without even noticing it, we found ourselves close to the other river. And finally our curiosity was satisfied. We boarded the Turk's yacht. It was large and new. The odor of tar greeted our noses, and despite the explanations the Arab gave us as to function of the sails, masts, and the endless coils of rope, we didn't understand a thing.

"Nazim Effendi received us in caftan and slippers in his sumptuous cabin near the foremast. Our eyes had never beheld such magnificent Oriental carpets, brass vessels, gold-embroidered cushions, and a huge collection of weapons: arquebuses, scimitars, pistols, Turkish swords, all filigreed with gold, silver and ivory. Unknown scents agreeably tickled our nostrils. The walls were covered with rugs, and in a place of honor, hung a portrait of the Sultan Abdul Medjid. Also resplendent were the other items: the national emblem of Turkey, verses from the Koran penned in elegant Arabic script, and portraits of beautiful and dazzling odalisques. The latter caught the eye of Kyra who exclaimed, 'How beautiful they are!'

"'You are also beautiful, Miss!' responded the Turk.

"We were served delicious baklava along with coffee presented in superbly fashioned Turkish cups. Next the hookahs were brought out, and we smoked delicately perfumed tobacco.

"Our host was courteous, gay and full of good cheer. He asked Kyra discreet questions about our parents, and she, without saying anything, said everything. She informed him that she had learned how to dance and loved it. Nazim Effendi, pleased with our visit, rose and escorted us to the launch. As we were leaving he said, 'You can dance here whenever you please.'

"And at that, we were taken back to the Romanian shore.

"I was happy and proud of my discovery of the Turk and suspected nothing. Kyra was even happier and as gullible. We surrendered our former way of life, all our old pursuits. Our life was now entirely given over to that fatal yacht. Each day we went out in the launch and only returned to the inn to sleep and eat. This seemed so much better! Kyra was now feeling that her wardrobe was not as fancy as it should be, and she found our rooms unbearable. She was hoping that our uncle Cosma would finish off our father so that she could return to the house and with her fortune, become an elegant lady, and receive not the *moussafirs* but Nazim Effendi. The poor girl!

"We spent a whole week on board the yacht, dancing in the cabin and enjoying ourselves. Kyra swore that the Turk was 'a true father.' He brought out from his coffers the most splendid Odalisque garments and laid them out for us to marvel at. One day, he even dressed my sister in one of the outfits. She became a true odalisque, just as in the paintings. So that I wouldn't feel neglected, he dressed me as a Turk, with a fez, billowing pants, and even stuck a pistol in my embroidered belt. Dressed like this, we were on the verge of asking that he raise the anchor and set sail.

"That's exactly what he finally did; but in the meantime, to toy with us, he undressed us, put the clothing back in his chests, and we went home for the evening with our mouths watering for more.

"The next morning—our last day on Romanian soil—Kyra cried from anger. Our father was still alive, and Uncle Cosma had not yet even fired a shot at him. But if he had been slow in doing his work for our benefit, others had been busy.

"Early that morning we heard a voice beneath our windows crying 'Fresh Crayfish. Crayfish.' We bounded down the stairs. Bent under the weight of his years, and no doubt of his sins, old Ibrahim turned away from our windows, as if he'd seen thieves. We caught up with him near Katagatz, and there, far from the port, he whispered nasally, 'I bring you awful news! Cosma was ambushed by your father's men and shot dead. His brother was wounded but escaped on his horse!'

"That whole morning we did nothing but weep uncontrollably. Our protector was dead! His *ursita* had told the truth: he had met death at the hand of his third enemy. What were we to do now? Our father, with no one now to fear, would surely come for us.

"We were gripped with mortal terror. It would be better to jump in the Danube than return to the inn! We headed to the river. There was the launch waiting for us. We reached the yacht in no time, and upon boarding we threw ourselves into the arms of Nazim Effendi as if we were his children.

"Kyra, her beautiful face awash in tears, told our new 'father' everything, including the last disaster that had befallen us. Finally, overcome by grief, she exclaimed, 'We'd rather throw ourselves in the river than return to the inn.'

"'There's no reason to feel so hopeless, my children,' said our smooth-tongued captor. You are both of Turkish ancestry, through your esteemed grandfather. I will take you to Stamboul where I'm certain your mother went to get her eye treated. We'll find her there, and then you'll be happy again.'

"He kissed us both.

"'How soon can we leave?' asked Kyra.

"'Within a few hours, once the sun goes down.'

"Happy in the midst of horror, we threw ourselves at his feet, and hugged his knees. He was our savior. And that night, with infernal clamor emanating from the port, we closed ourselves up in the cabin where we smoked *cubuks* filled with opium. Our heads spun with hallucinations, and we floated in a fog where nothingness coexisted with happiness. Suddenly we felt the cabin begin to rock in a way that we thought we were ascending to heaven.

"But we weren't going to heaven. We were on our way to Stamboul where we believed we'd find our mother and bring her back home. Where we were really going was into captivity and of our own free will.

"Another day I will tell you the odyssey of my peregrinations in search of my sister, who was locked up in a harem on our arrival in Constantinople. As for me, I had to yield to the pleasure of our respectable benefactor and was corrupted forever. And Kyra was lost to me for all time. I was enslaved for two years, then spent another twelve searching for her, supporting myself by selling salep.

Fourteen years later, on returning to Romania, I learned that not long after we had fled, the uncle who had cheated death took revenge for us all. He set on fire both of the houses—that of my mother and that of my father—to make sure my father wouldn't escape. And this time he didn't miss: my father was burned alive."

Book III:
Dragomir

Four years had streamed by since Adrien had heard Stavro tell his tales about Kyra. Despite his inquiries and attempts to find the blighted lemonade seller so that he might demonstrate how fond and friendly he was of him, he hadn't had any luck. Stavro had disappeared, and Adrien thought he was dead. It was not that Adrien's life had stopped; on the contrary. In following his own destiny this passionate young man had himself piled up plenty of adventures.

This destiny suited him fine, at least in terms of what interested him most in life: the need to look ceaselessly into the deepest part of the human soul. The multitude of nameless beings he encountered rarely possessed souls worth exploring, but Adrien knew how to find them, and by chance he occasionally came upon them.

One evening, extremely bored in Cairo, where he had been residing for a month, Adrien turned his footsteps toward Darb-el-Barabra Street and entered a cosmopolitan Jewish-Romanian café, frequented by all sorts of people, with all sorts of morals, from all walks of life. There was no affinity among Mr. Goldstein's customers; they distrusted one another, and frequently even hated each other. They did agree, however, on two things: the stuffed pike and the Romanian *tzouika*—plum brandy. When Adrien had enough to pay for these items, he ordered them, and that evening he could. But his distaste for the clientele was obvious. To avoid having to get into an unwanted conversation with someone he'd rather not, he lowered his head, and without acknowledging the other's presence, made a retreat for the back of the room. Here, where the tables were bare of tablecloths, the downtrodden working men gathered. From there he could listen to the conversations around him while observing the crowd.

"How that man resembles Stavro!" he said to himself while eating his pike with his fingers and furtively glancing at the man seated in profile in the corner opposite him.

The man was poorly dressed, with a month-old beard, and advanced in age. He sat still, with his chin resting on his palm, his eyes nonchalantly gazing at the doorway, with a glass of *tzouïka* under his nose. His looks did not attract attention and yet Adrien, though he found it hard to believe that Stravro could be in Egypt, found his heart going out to this lonely old man, who sat silent and impassive. Adrien would have liked to be able to see his face from the front, but the man didn't move and seemed almost numb. Adrien decided to make use of the Oriental custom of buying a drink for someone one didn't know who was either of the same class or lower, purely for the sake of doing a good deed. He called the waiter over and asked him to serve a glass of *tzouïka* to the man sitting in the corner, thinking that this would lead to an exchange of thankfulness and good wishes. But instead, to his great surprise, he saw the man refuse the drink that he himself had not ordered.

"It was ordered by that man over there," said the waiter, motioning toward Adrien.

"So what," said the man, without even bothering to glance at Adrien.

It was his voice that gave him away. Adrien was now sure it was Stavro who sat across from him, and he went over, full of emotion, and touched his shoulder. He couldn't find his full voice, so he leaned over and whispered in his ear:

"Is it possible? Is it you? Here?"

"Didn't you already know it?" Stavro replied, looking at him without any surprise in his face.

"What?" responded Adrien, somewhat annoyed. "You saw me come in and you didn't even bother to greet me. And then you refused my drink when the waiter brought it. So what's with you? Have you become a monster these last years?"

"One becomes something like that toward the end of a life like I've had. Kindness isn't sufficient any longer."

"But my feelings for you are only kind. And yours for me?"

"I'm only talking about the kindness in drinks, or the kindness of offering someone a drink. As for you…"

"What about me?"

"Well, you are climbing the great hill of life whereas I'm heading down the other side, and between us is the summit. And then…" Stavro stopped speaking, and looked around him with suspicion.

"Aren't you hungry, Stavro?" asked Adrien, warmly.

"Yes, I'm hungry."

"Would you like some stuffed pike? They make it nicely here."

"Pike, toad or elephant, order whatever you want. But I'd like something a little kinder than a glass of *tzouika*. I can even buy that for myself." And in a gesture of weariness, Stavro rubbed his wrinkled face.

An hour later, Stavro sat in front of a glass of wine in Adrien's little room, lighted by a gas lamp. Warmed anew by the kindness of his young friend, Stavro burned his last drops of oil in fueling that sacred internal flame that sustains the soul of passionate men.

"Now that I've brought you up to date on my latest and most grotesque doings—that of making do while dying of hunger—I know, my dear Adrien, that only your sensitivity toward my state of being keeps you from asking about what happened to Kyra, or better yet, to tell you the story of little Dragomir, as I was called then. I would like, for your sake, to go back in time to that tumultuous part of my life. But you need to know that one still suffers when he digs around in the suitcases from long-ago trips.

"I was almost fifteen when I finally freed myself from Nazim Effendi's boat which was docked in Constantinople. I was beautiful, I was stupid, and I was dressed and decked out like the son of a Turkish prince. According to my abductor, my clothes alone were worth the price of a fine Arabian horse. My watch had been ordered especially for me and custom made by the Sultan's watchmaker. The rings on all my fingers were jeweled; my fez was entirely embroidered in gold thread. And what's more, my pockets bulged with heavy handfuls of Turkish pounds. I could have lived on just this money for ten years without having to lift a finger.

"But money alone isn't enough to make a life. My soul ached terribly, my heart was extremely innocent, and because I was also sentimental, I was the victim of both my heart and soul. I was in pain because of my longing for Kyra and my mother, now both lost to me, and so essential for my being able to live. My innocence of heart made me believe that when at last I was free people would help me find them, and to find them, I was prepared to sacrifice all and everything. I was, without even realizing it, sacrificing my own body, now corrupted, now used to this new way of being. One gets accustomed to everything in life but one accommodates vice more easily than any other awful thing. It is true that when I was a prisoner I said to myself more than once that had only Kyra and Mama been there, I wouldn't have asked for anything better than the life I was leading!

"I was so happy at seeing myself miraculously escape from my gilded prison that—Lord God pardon me—I did forget for a bit about Kyra and my mother! I was no longer in fear of my tyrant. While his yacht was anchored off Constantinople, he let down his guard, and one night I was able to set foot ashore. For a long time, until dawn, I ran along the docks facing the Bosphorus cursing him and defiantly shaking the splayed fingers of my hand in his direction.

"'Go to hell, you perfumed pervert! And may God in all His grace send upon you a wild storm when you are alone in your evil boat under the sky of the Black Sea! And may all the fish at the bottom of the sea feast on your swollen corpse! Amen!'

"Now that the nightmare of being on that boat had disappeared, a dizzy joy swept over me, and I ran in every direction along the dirty streets of the Galata district, stepping on the tails of innumerable mangy dogs, colliding with salep sellers, knocking down blind pilgrims and turning over the hookahs of smokers seated on the sidewalks. I had new eyes and a freedom I had never known. The passersby thought me mad, and a bailiff stopped me and, without touching, greeted me with utmost respect and said to me in words so polite they made me laugh,'May I say to you, son of a bey, that it is unwise of your father to allow you to amuse yourself like this! What is your illustrious name? Who is your tutor?'

"'Why do you say 'illustrious' and 'tutor?'" I asked him, pulling up my breeches that had fallen to my knees.

"And without waiting for another word, I turned my back on him. A man on horseback came by at a trot, trailed by the horse's owner who had grabbed onto its tail. I found this quite funny and did the same until I lost my breath and had to let go.

That first day of freedom was the only time I was completely happy in those days. I was carefree and without any worries. I wanted to do a thousand things at the same time: cross the bridges, go to the Golden Horn, take in the women who belly danced in the brothels, climb the steep streets up to the Pera district. I finally decided to go horseback riding, and I chose the most beautiful horse I could find. The owner was receptive and courteous. He helped me mount and adjusted the stirrups for my height. He quickly realized I had no idea how to ride, nor what route I wanted to take, and he patiently instructed me how to hold the reins, and asked where I wanted to go.

"'Everywhere,' I said, standing up in the stirrups.

"'Everywhere?' he responded, astonished. 'But your lordship cannot go everywhere at the same time. You have to choose a path.'

"'All right,' I replied. 'Set me on a course that will take me to those hills that cast their reflection on the Bosphorus.'

"We set off, with him guiding me, toward the Sultan's Palace—the Yildiz Kiosk—and the Dolmabahce Palace. I was dazzled by these sites that filled my head with the most fantastic unreality. During the long and sweet hours that we spent there, with my horse gently bouncing me in the saddle, I was awestruck by the marvels that passed in front of my half-closed eyes. My body, my soul, my real being was transported into another world. My entire past vanished. I forgot the man who led the animal by its bridle and who did not say a word. I didn't say a word either, not even to ask a question, during the entire sojourn. I only awakened a bit from my dream state when the horse stopped and a voice I did not know entered my euphoria, 'Effendi, it is late. It will soon be night. And I'm hungry, and my horse, also. May I take you to the door of your residence?'

"I understood that I should dismount, and I did, but I was dizzy. In my legs, a painful sensation made me lose my balance, and I sat down on the ground.

"'Would you like to stay here?' asked my guide. I shook my head yes and pulled out of my pocket a gold Turkish pound that I gave to him. I knew I had to pay him but I had no idea what money was worth, nor what things cost.

"'You owe me three *chereks*. You don't by any chance have them, do you?' I dug in my pocket and handed him two more gold coins.

"'No, no Effendi, you're giving me far too much, and I can't make change.'

"'It's all right. Keep the gold coin.'

"'I can't do that. I don't make that much in a week.'

"'It's nothing to me,' I said. 'Keep it.'

"'By Allah, no!' he practically shouted. 'Your powerful father could have my head cut off if I accepted that much!'

"At that he took out every coin he had in his kémir, and piled in front of me an enormous number of coins: *medjidies, chereks, bechliks* and *meteliks*.

Bowing, he said farewell with an Asalaam 'Alaykum, got on his horse, and rode off.

I sat alone on the rich green grass alongside the beautiful road that bordered the sea. I fixed my gaze on the calm water, overwhelmed by the extraordinary images that could have been drawn directly from the most fantastic Oriental tales. The fabulous palaces surrounded by pine groves gleamed in half light, and the setting sun projected their elongated reflections onto the mirrored surface of the Bosphorus. And the sky was awash in an array of color. Streaks of brilliant gold, copper and red flamed across the horizon, framing in relief the hills with their purple crests looming over the sea.

"Was the rest of the earth so beautiful? I hadn't known it at all. I was seeing the world for the first time. Mama's salon and Nazim Effendi's floating prison had comprised my whole life up until then. I was so totally dazed by that remarkable day, and so lost in reverie provoked by the splendid twilight, that by the time a boat passed near me with a rower singing a beautiful and melancholic song, it was almost night. Where was I? And what should I eat? And where were Kyra and Mama? Where should I head now?

Sobs began to form in my chest, cries rose from my throat, and warm tears started to flow down my cheeks. The rower heard me and looked toward me, but when he was not more than a couple of yards from the dock, he took a look at me, and exclaimed in Greek: 'Oh, my soul! You can't be as miserable as you seem. You're covered in gold!"

"I've known since that night that you can't always trust a beautiful voice.

"The road back to town was so lonely that I allowed myself to call out in distress. I was a young man delivered into a world without pity. Neither the gold bursting from my pockets, nor the precious rings on my fingers, nor the pocket watch fit for a prince could console me. In my eyes, their value was already compromised. I owed everything down to my underclothes to that man who had abducted me. If not Kyra, if not my mother, then just a lock of their hair would have been worth more to me than all this ill-gotten metal. A lock of hair would have done more for my heart than all those precious stones.

"I pressed my burning face against each tree along the dark road, wetting their rough bark with my tears. I hugged each trunk, railing against their indifference to my fate. Into the night I mouthed repeatedly 'Mama! Mama! Mama! Kyra! Mama! Where are you? I am free! And I don't know where to go. And it's night. And the world is so large, with so many people. But there is no Kyra, no Mama.'

When I turned the corner my eyes were met by a powerful light. Two men, their legs naked, carrying flaming torches in their hands ran rapidly by crying out in a single voice, 'Look out.'

"I barely had time to move before a horse and rich carriage roared by, and a whip cracked in the night air. At the same moment, I felt a sharp searing pain in my neck and on my chin. I fell to the ground, my face down in the grass. I had not felt such terrible pain since the brutal days when I was thrashed by my father and brother.

"I got up gradually and with difficulty, blind with pain. The road was now even darker than before, and I was seized by a frightful panic. I set off running as fast as my legs could carry me, speechless, afraid of everything even my own breathing, the wind whipping past my ears. Houses and streets, both clean and dirty, began to appear, as did people and street peddlers, and dogs that grudgingly moved out of the way, and finally, in an empty lot, I collapsed in a faint.

"I was awakened by a man who was trying to help me sit up. Under the moonlight, he looked like Ibrahim, the Katagatz crayfish fisherman, and hope stirred in my heart that I might find my sister and mother. I threw my arms around his grimy neck, which reeked of sweat and tobacco, and began to sob, 'I've lost my sister and mother, and I'm miserable. Help me to find them and I'll give you all the gold in my pockets, all my rings and my watch and my clothes…'

"'By Allah, don't cry out like that!' the old man said sternly, as he covered my mouth with his wet hand.

"He helped me up and told me to come with him. As we begin to walk I noticed that he carried on his arm a basket of Turkish Delight. The old peddler and I walked for more than a half hour, which totally exhausted me. Until that night I had never waded through so much mud, my eyes had never seen so many filthy and frightfully miserable neighborhoods. Finally, he led me into a room behind a small shop where there was nothing but a wretched straw bed and a jug of water, both on the floor. That was all; absolutely all.

"'Tell me your story, now,' he said, as he set down his basket and sat Turkish-style on the bed.

"In less than an hour I recounted my tale of woe, and while I made it brief I didn't keep anything from him. I began by telling about life at my mother's house and ended with my slipping off the yacht. He listened without saying a word. At the end, he got up. "You can sleep there,' he said, motioning to the bed. 'That's all I can say tonight.'

"I was a little taken aback by his brusqueness but firmly convinced that he would help me find the two I loved most in the world. I let myself fall heavily onto the bed, and as I was drifting into sleep I could see my benefactor crouching in the corner of the room, his eyes fixed on me.

"We got up early the next morning.

"'It's time to leave,' he said.

"'To find Kyra?' I asked, quickly.

"'No, my child, not to find Kyra. And I must never see you again for your gold, your jewels and your clothes are cursed. May Allah come to your aid!'

"He closed the door behind us, and with his basket under his arm walked away.

"This old man, as well as the bailiff, the boatman and the man who rented horses were the best four people, and the only honest ones, I would meet for a long time. And that first day of freedom remains the only day I can remember when my heart was not heavy. From then on, my moves sent me straight into the abyss.

"I was so stupefied by being cruelly abandoned by the Turkish Delight seller, whom I decided was simply mad, that I couldn't even summon the strength to weep. My mind refused to believe that everyone was so mean spirited, and my first thought was to find someone with a heart less hardened. Life, I decided, was waiting to show me a miracle.

"I don't know what kind of bizarre infantile thinking persuaded me that my mother was still getting her eye taken care of in a local hospital, but I decided that I should begin investigating at once. With this idea in my head, I began walking, asking passersby how to get to the center of town. Everybody directed me toward Pera, where I arrived an hour before mid-day.

"I was so hungry I could barely stand, so I looked for a place to eat on a side street from which wafted the beckoning smell of roasted mutton. On the corner, in front of a little café, a man was fanning a charcoal grill on which kebabs were cooking. He wore a fez, and his opened shirt revealed a bronzed, hairy chest. He turned from side to side, rolling his eyes and crying out, 'Kebab! Kebab!'

"I went into the café, which had no customers, and ordered bread and a kebab. On a dirty wooden table, I devoured about a half loaf of bread, three spits of meat, and drank water. When I went to pay, I stuck out my hand full of gold, silver and copper pieces and told the proprietor to take what he needed as payment for the meal. The man stepped back, looked me over, glanced about left and right, and then snatched a gold piece and stuck it quickly in his caftan. On leaving I said to myself that a meal here either costs far more than a whole day of riding or else this swindler was not worried about 'getting his head cut off by my father.'

"Impatient with desire to find a friendly man who would put himself generously at my service, I walked directly to the biggest café in the square. I thought to myself that it was smarter to ask help from folks who were well off or even aristocrats since they would not have the need to rob me, nor be afraid of my clothes or money.

"My reasoning was correct. But before entering, I followed the suit of many others with shoes as mud-caked as mine, and put my foot up on the box of a man shining shoes. And this time I was shrewder; I watched how much others were paying the shoeshine man, and like them, I gave him the smallest of small coins, a *métélik*. Then, with my shoes gleaming, I entered.

"A roar of voices, of tossed dice and of backgammon pieces slapped down on game boards created a nearly overwhelming cacophony of sound. There were practically no empty seats at the tables, and everyone was playing some sort of game. Everyone seemed distinguished whether they were nobles, government officials or military officers. I walked the length of the room twice but no one, not even a waiter, paid attention to me despite my rich attire.

"'How nice it is to be among only well educated people,' I thought to myself. 'I feel far more at ease here than among the poor on the street.'

"I finally found a free chair next to two chess players. I ordered a coffee with cream and a hookah. Again I paid attention to how much others were paying for their drinks, and to my great astonishment I discovered that a single piece of silver could buy ten coffees and many hookahs, with the tip included.

"I looked at the two chess players who were sitting next to me. One was an officer, the other a civilian. Both were young and totally absorbed in their game. I took to them both, particularly the officer who was sitting next to me. He had a rather stern face and didn't speak much, but when he did it was in exquisite Turkish. This pleased me but at the same time made my heart shiver: Nazim Effendi spoke equally well. The officer's uniform with his chest decorated with medals, however, reassured me that he must be good. I leaned toward him and said, 'Excuse me sir but can you tell me...' He raised his index finger without looking at me, stopping me in midsentence. I decided that my approach was not successful because I was being overly familiar, or too confident, so a little later I leaned over to question him again. Before I could open my mouth he stopped me with the same gesture and with the other hand moved one of the chess pieces. I was not going to be silenced, and renewed my entreaty, "'Excuse me sir. Do you know where they take people to have their eyes fixed after they've been put out?'

"'Whose eyes have been put out?' he said so loudly and gruffly that I recoiled with fear.

"'My, my mother,' I stammered.

"'Your mother had her eyes put out? And who put them out?" he asked, looking me over from head to toe.

"'Not both of them,' I said timidly. 'Just one'

"'Who did it? When? How?'

"'My father did it when he beat her up, in Brăila, in Romania. It was two years ago.'

"'The officer seemed exasperated. He turned toward his friend and repeated what I had said. 'A woman who was beaten up in Romania two years ago and had her eye put out is being sought today in Constantinople. Can you understand anything of that, Mustafa?'

"'Oh yes, yes, I understand,' said the other man. 'We'll have to look into it, but away from here.'

"He caressed my cheek and added, 'First, we must put this child at ease.'

"We left the café. Once outside he hailed a taxi and the three of us got in.

"Six months of sweet hope and cruel deception, of relative freedom and a life of opulence followed this second and last encounter with generous rich men who spoke exquisite Turkish.

"When we got to Mustafa bey's door, the officer took leave of his friend. Before leaving, he gave me a severe and contemptuous look. I did not see him again for a number of years, in circumstances I'll tell you about later. I judged him harshly, and in my childish enthusiasm, I said to the bey, 'He's very haughty, your friend.'

"'Yes, he's haughty, but good.' (And to think that Mustafa bey spoke of kindness!)

"His house was a huge villa on the southern outskirts of the city. It was surrounded by an enormous park that stretched all the way to the Bosphorus. It was silent in the richly furnished interior and full of invisible servants as mute as tombstones. But the intimacy of the rooms, common to those in all Oriental houses, made me feel comfortable. The extreme delicacy of the bey contributed to my ease. He didn't have any of Nazim's treachery. As long as my hope lasted, he was charming, irresistible, and polite. I would have nothing to reproach him about today, not even his inability to satisfy my impossible desire, had he, when my hopes fell, simply shown me the door. But so tyrannical is Oriental passion that it subverts even the most generous heart, and replaces goodness with either malice or violence. And both are wicked.

"Mustafa knew more about me and my past than anyone has since. I am convinced he was sincerely touched by my story, for more than once when I told him my tale of woe, his eyes filled with tears.

"He promised he would do everything possible, 'If your mother can be found in Constantinople, we'll find her,' he told me, as he caressed my hands. 'I'll inquire at the police and at the hospitals. As for Kyra, I will send some female intermediaries, as subtle as ether and as sly as foxes, into the most diligently guarded harems. If she's discovered, I guarantee we'll get her out. With gold everything can be gotten in Turkey.'

"He showed me to my rooms and ordered a servant to be at my service. He replaced my jewels and clothes, which he considered 'too ostentatious, even indecent,' with others that were more 'dignified.' In exchange for his taking care of me he imposed only one condition: that I not frequent the large cafés nor often go into the city.

"'It's in your best interest,' he said. 'Nazim will not easily surrender his prey, and you might find yourself one day with a hood around you, tied up, and tossed onto his boat like a simple sack of *yenibahar*—allspice.'

"This possibility filled me with terror. As a result, I felt myself comfortable with him and with the relative freedom I saw opening before my young adolescent eyes.

"There are several ways to deliver a passionate soul into ruin. The easiest is to talk to them tenderly. And as at that time, I was preoccupied with thoughts of Kyra, Mustafa bey not only drew me out about her, he also added his own thoughts.

"It was all done quite naturally, for he was sincerely fond of me. But the devil can have his type of sincere passion. More often than not, passion is nothing more than an intoxicating drug.

"Mustafa bey began calling things I liked by Kyra's name. As 'hookah' and 'bracelet,' in Romanian, are feminine nouns, he brought me the most beautiful hookah I have ever seen, followed by an expensive bracelet. On both of them, he had engraved the word 'Kyra.' But I couldn't read the word because it was written in Ottoman script. And I had barely been in his house for a month when one day, on his grounds, he came holding by its bridle a beautiful mare as young, lissome, capricious and impatient as Kyra herself.

"'Take her,' he told me. 'Here is the most beautiful Kyralina that I can offer you. She's yours!'

"He quickly helped me to mount her and acquainted me with her unique movements. Mustafa and my servant mounted their own horses, and with me riding between them, we took off to explore the picturesque land to the north of his villa.

"I'm certain, and take some consolation in knowing that during that entire brief period in which I lived so opulently, I never forgot for more than three days running how disastrous my childhood had been. To be sure, there was no way in which my poor heart was immune from the intoxication of this life. How could I resist? Nourished by the words of hope that the bey constantly uttered, my days were taken up with my hookah and my mare. She was a wonderful animal, whom I left only to eat and sleep. Her temperament was her own, with its likes and dislikes, and it didn't take me long to believe that she was channeling, in some way, Kyra's love for me. She was as devoted to me as I to her, and if I stayed inside with the bey playing backgammon, the noble beast would make her displeasure known by noisily stamping her feet in the stable.

"The beautiful black eyes of the horse were Kyra's. Kyra was present in my personal objects, in our conversation, and was very much a part of the household. As for the intermediaries who were sent to find her, they continually brought me assurances, one more convinced than the other, that Kyra was living in ten harems at the same time.

"Their astonishingly exact descriptions, including detailed descriptions of the girl they had spied, made my heart leap, then dance with joy. I gobbled up their words like a six-year-old child, and wrapped my arms around many of their necks, crying out, 'That's her! That's my sister! Try to approach her and speak my name: Dragomir. And do everything you can get a picture of her.'

"But to speak to those in the harem, to obtain a photograph, to close curious eyes, to deafen the ears of the indiscreet, to open well-guarded doors, required money—a great deal of money.

"In the middle of the room stood the bey, his hands in his pockets, his eyes sneaky and filled with irony, listening and smiling. I fell to his feet and implored him to help me. He generously distributed pieces of silver, according to how important each member of the harem was.

"Long days of waiting, each filled with sad and painful hours followed, and I felt completely enervated. In my hopelessness I sought refuge in Kyralina, whose spirit was undaunted. I rode her with my arms around her silky neck, in the morning sunshine, or at evening when the sky blazed with color, but I was often so overwhelmed with nostalgia for days past that not even these rides could cheer me up.

"At my side my servant always rode, armed to the teeth, never letting me get more than a foot in front of him. His silence, his lack of friendliness, his incomprehension of my fate, wounded me.

"In this way spring flowed into summer, and summer into autumn. But it wasn't until September that my hopes abruptly crashed. The photos the women brought me were not of Kyra, and the name Dragomir, whispered into the ears of these miserable captives, did not echo in the dark labyrinth of their hearts. I gave up listening to the sweet words these women continued to utter and showed them the door.

"Bad luck is often followed by more bad luck, and so it was. The investigations into whether my mother might be in Constantinople, turned up not even the slimmest lead. Pressed by my questions, the bey brought in the chief of the Turkish police to prove that he was doing all he could to find her. The police chief was huge, with a face like a murderer. He had a long mustache and the eyes of a bandit. He stamped his feet, and cried out in a voice so loud it almost knocked me over, 'Since Stamboul has existed, a Romanian woman with one eye has never set one foot down here.'

"He was more than convincing. Hopelessness swept over me and any illusion I may have had vanished. My tears flowed into the perfume-scented hands of the bey who tried to console. I begged him to let me go, but he wouldn't.

"'What would become of you if you left here? You're as dumb as a sheep. Even more, you have the misfortune of being young and handsome, two qualities that have never brought good fortune to anyone in Turkey unless he is wily, and you are not. Stay here. In my house you have everything you need, and far more than one of your birth could ever hope for.'

"'I was devastated. His words rang in my ears like a death knell. But the bey redoubled his efforts. Knowing my love for horseback riding, he ordered a hunting outfit for me, and bought me a beautiful rifle, its stock engraved. The bey christened it 'The terrible Kyra'. And so outfitted and equipped, we set out one morning, accompanied by two servants, along the main road to Andrinopole.

"'I want to show you some deer and vultures,' he said. 'And you will see that life is beautiful, even without a woman. What you don't know is that the most beautiful woman always ends up as a whore.

"This insult pierced me like a dagger, and Mustafa bey was now odious in my eyes. I hid my feelings, but once we were in the field, I hatched an escape plan.

"A marvelous opportunity soon presented itself when we were on a two-week hunting trip that the bey took each fall to the nearest Balkan states along the Maritza River. I had three different plans. The first was to take advantage of a lack of vigilance on the part of the servants, and flee disguised as a Turkish peasant. The second strategy was to buy my freedom from the attendants. And if the first two were not possible, I had a third, rather desperate plan of escape: to make use of the swift legs of Kyralina. According to the bey, the horse could run extremely well. To convince myself of this, I asked Moutapha if he would allow me to race her against his horse. As he was happy to see me in good humor, he accepted and agreed to give me a three hundred pace lead. He would follow quickly behind, hoping to catch up with me in a village visible about three kilometers away.

"A pistol shot from the bey's gun was the signal for me to dig my spurs into Kyralina's flanks. The mare reared on her hind legs, chomped down on the bit, and took off like the wind. I let out the reins and settled myself into the saddle. The wind whistled past my ears with such force that I tried in vain to hear the galloping strides of my rival. I had no idea how much ground I might be losing, and I kicked furiously. The earth churned under Kyralina's hooves, and the gray road appeared to be enchanted.

The village soon came into view, but to the astonishment of the inhabitants, I didn't slacken my pace. Geese, chickens and ducks that were unable to get out of the road were trampled under the horse's hooves.

Finally, about a kilometer on the other side, the bey caught up with me. A little afterward the servants arrived, toting my rifle that I didn't even know I had lost.

"'You won,' said the bey, as he shook my hand. 'Tell me what you want, and I'll give it to you.'

"'Very well,' I said, give me a kilometer's lead and promise not to look for me if you don't overtake me by the time I reach the next village.'

"He seemed upset, 'Do you hate me that much? What are you lacking? Women? You can have as many as you want; in my harem I've got fourteen-year-old virgins. They're from every country, of every skin color, of every race. And the most they ask for is to be our slaves, since otherwise they would end up one day with some imbecile.'

"'Mustafa bey,' I cried. 'Don't you believe that freedom is far better than slavery, and that an 'imbecile' that one loves is worth more than a prince one detests?'

"'That's right,' he replied. 'But don't be so concerned with what is right. Focus on what is good. We are the absolute masters of all on earth, animals included. We take, therefore, what is stupidly offered to our power!'

"At that instant my eyes were opened, and I suddenly had a new sense of what life was about. The bey, though cynical, was right: the weak offer everything stupidly to those who have power. They don't even have to be forced to do it.

"In Turkey or in Bulgaria, whether Muslims or Christians, rich or poor, all were docile slaves. And if a young girl hid herself at our arrival, her father, to enter into the good graces of the powerful, would think nothing of sacrificing her in the same way he would offer us his best bed and his finest sheep.

"This awakening made me want my freedom even more. I felt myself guilty at leading such an opulent life; in my young heart the need was being born to find an independent trade that would allow me to put bread on the table in an honest fashion. From that moment on nothing interested me except escaping. But such an occasion did not present itself that day, and that evening I was even unhappier than I had been.

"I was carefully watched. During the day I was made to go on long and tiring hunts, always flanked by either the bey or his servants. At night I slept in the room of my protector, without any hope of escape. As a result, the first of my schemes collapsed, and the second—to buy my freedom—was also rendered impossible.

One day during a torrential downpour, while the bey was playing chess with his host at the inn, I found myself equally engaged in a game of backgammon with my servant. We were alone. To get what I wanted, I became tender and sentimental and expressed my desire to escape. He gave me a deaf ear. I then offered him my gold and jewels but he refused them.

"'Isn't it true, Ahmed, that gold will buy everything in Turkey?'

"'Yes, that's true.' he murmured. 'But he who gets the gold must get enough to save his head, and you don't have enough.'

"All that I could do now was to attempt to put my desperate third plan of flight into action. I knew that I might be killed like a dog, but that didn't make me hesitate for a minute.

"We were now in a mountainous and forested region that was conducive to making my scheme work. Very early the next morning we began ascending a difficult route through a pine forest. Five men on horseback were with us in order to flush prey from the woods. In order not to give my servant time to inform his master of my proposition of the night before, I decided to take my chances at the first possible opportunity. And that opportunity came quickly.

"We stopped at the edge of a clearing. Below was a little lake into which a waterfall gushed. 'The chamois come to drink here,' our guide said calmly.

"He set off with the other four beaters. The two servants took up posts at two strategic points with orders to fire at any given moment so as to drive the game into range of the bey's rifle. With the group scattered, I could see my freedom coming into view as it was much easier to escape from one man than from a group.

"We were hidden in the crevice of a rock from which we could see the open ground through which the game would be driven.

"'Don't fire unless you see I miss my target, or unless a chamois passes right in front of your nose,' said Mustafa bey. 'Kyra the Terrible is not so terrible in your hands.'

"He was right. I had no idea how to shoot.

"An hour went by, maybe even two or three, before a shot rang out, then two or three more. The bey, his rifle ready, ran his eyes over the scene, and suddenly, as if the sun had come out, a beautiful stag leapt straight into our path. But within a second, he disappeared in Ahmede's direction.

"'We'll get him!' the bey yelled. 'I'll head him off. You stay here and guard the passage, in case he turns back toward the road.'

"'Stay yourself,' I said. 'And what's more, here's your rifle,' I yelled, hurling his gun after him as he galloped away.

"I threw down my musette bag and my rifle and cut through the gap into the valley. Quitting the road, I rode toward the dense pine forest. I quickly came upon a good road and spurred the mare onward. My life and freedom depended on her speed.

"'Kyra's namesake, my love, help me!' I implored the horse as I threw my arms around her neck.

"I must have gone five leagues or so from the site of the hunt before I stopped on the banks of the Maritza. The autumn sky was resplendently lit. I let the mare graze and rest while I, crippled with fatigue and filled with high hopes, stretched out on the grass. But a sense of fear came over me as I realized that in my mad dash for freedom I had been seen by people in villages and by woodcutters on the side of the road. I asked myself over and over 'Am I free or not?'

"I looked out at the vast and beautiful land in front of me, and pondered whether it was safe to sleep, or whether I should get up and go on foot. The shadow of an invisible hand menaced me; it could at any moment seize me by the collar and do with me what it would.

"Sleep quickly came to hold me in its embrace. My eyelids closed. When they opened again, I saw a very different scene from when I had fallen asleep. Mustafa bey was sitting at my side, watching me. He showed me a little doeskin sack, and said, as I rubbed my eyes to erase the nightmare, 'Here, Dragomir, I brought your lunch. You must be hungry.'

"And within minutes we were back on our horses.

"'Ah,' he exclaimed. 'You wanted to play with me a little, didn't you? Don't you know that what God forgets, a Muslim takes?

"A few days later when we returned to Constantinople, the first words of the bey to his two servants were these: 'You are to accompany Dragomir for a ride on horseback two times a week for an hour, and always at a trot, but pay close attention to him. At the first sign of an escape, I order you to shoot the mare out from under him.'

"And to me he said, 'Within the house you are free only to wander at will around your own rooms!'

"The servants did not find it too difficult to follow his orders since that same day I became quite ill and was confined to bed. For an entire week I was unconscious and delirious from a high fever.

"When I began to recover, I found my room transformed into a real infirmary. Two doctors took turns watching over me. Mustafa bey was panic-stricken, and forgetting his exalted status, he knelt at my bed to beg my forgiveness.

"'Will you allow me to leave?' I asked.

"'That, my dearest one, I cannot do. Ask me for something else, whatever you'd like!'

"'All right, then. Let me die!' I said, and turned my face to the wall.

"I really did want to die. But one can't die by wishing it. Three weeks later I finally was able to get out of bed and entered into a month-long convalescence marked by states of extreme anxiety and numbing depression.

"Every present that the bey brought me I destroyed in a rage. I threw my beautiful hookah against the bars of my window, and smashed the bracelet to pieces. Finally, I took to ripping up my clothes as soon as the tyrant's shadow entered my room.

"I did find one distraction during this time that unexpectedly and innocently began to restore some order to my being. It was winter, the sweet and sensual winter of the Bosphorus. Alone in my room from morning to night, I spent a good deal of my time looking out the three large windows in my downstairs sitting room that opened onto the bey's private park. To bring more life into the deserted park, I threw out scraps of food from my meals—bread, fruit, and meat—with the goal of attracting birds. It didn't take long for me to have under the window a number of sparrows and even a crow which had come to pick furtively through the tidbits.

"One day to my astonishment, a large dog appeared under the trees. He stayed a respectful distance away from the windows and sniffed the air, but when I called him he put his tail between his legs and sadly walked away.

"I thought to myself, 'He, too, must have had a taste of man's tenderness.'

"But in the days that followed he returned, and each time came a little closer. Because I didn't want to frighten him, I kept myself hidden but did toss out at least three quarters of my large meals to him. Little by little he began to get accustomed to me. When I spoke soft words to him he would respond by wagging the end of his tail but would quickly retreat. It was evident that it would take some time for him to trust me. I understood, having decided that I would also be cautious about choosing friends in the future should heaven help me to regain my freedom.

"This dog had a distinguished bearing. Even though hungry he ate with delicacy, seemingly vexed at having to eat his food off the ground. He chewed slowly and never gnawed a bone. He must surely be bearing a grudge. Why, for example, didn't he appeal to the pity of people to get some food? I knew that in Constantinople every Muslim has street dogs that accompany him every day to the bakery where he gets for them their pieces of bread. Maybe he found this practice less than honorable. Perhaps wandering the countryside to get a bit of food by himself was more to his liking. Or maybe the abject domesticity of his fellow canines was distasteful to him.

"I called him 'Wolf,' a name that I felt fit his wild and dignified life, and I was extremely careful in nurturing our budding friendship. My philosophy is that everyone is marked by suffering in his own way, and I respected his reserve. To prove to him that I understood who he was I did not throw his meat directly onto the ground but wrapped it in paper. He probably noticed this, because for the first time he decided to sit with his hind legs on the ground and look directly into my face, albeit at a stick's distance away.

"Wolf was a mongrel, completely brown, and solidly built. As to his hygiene, he did what he could. His large, sad black eyes were always somewhat closed, a result, I decided, of the hardships he had to endure, but their expression was difficult to decipher. In any case, they were neither tender nor indulgent. I reproached him directly for his cold serenity and his calm stubbornness.

"'Poor Wolf,' I told him, as I despairingly stuck my arm through the bars of the window in what I hoped was a sign that I trusted him. 'My poor Wolf, have you suffered so much that it has made your heart hard? I would like to believe that in the past you, too, had to endure the reversals of affection of the rich and powerful, that you also were given a hookah, bracelet, horse and rifle, and that you were sick and had doctors attending you. But now you are free, while I sit sick and hopeless behind these window bars. Come, brother Wolf, come near and let me pet you.'

"I don't want to pretend that in Turkey dogs speak Romanian, but it is true that my Wolf, after hearing my words for several long weeks, one day came and quite bravely put his paw in my hand. And that handshake was the most sincere one I've ever received in my life.

"I was happy, or at least I began to feel the benefits of a joy that only reposes in immortal hearts, and that has the power of overcoming sorrow. But I was careful not to betray my friendship with Wolf. In order that he not betray himself, I got him to understand that there would be nothing to eat when the windows were closed. He clearly understood this; if he found the windows closed he would simply make a half turn around the grounds and then leave. He also understood when I said to him, 'Go on, now, my friend, and come back and see me tomorrow.' He would leave as soon as I had closed the window, with no sign that he was at all upset or annoyed.

"Mustafa bey and his servants would come to visit me regularly. But seeing my state of anxiety, they would never stay long. The presence of the bey, in particular, set me off. As a result, he would barely enter the room so as not to create further disturbance. His rooms were next to mine with a large smoking room in between. To feel more secure, I locked the door into the smoking room.

"The joy I found in Wolf helped me feel calmer, and I became less anxious in the presence of the bey who responded to my improved state by rewarding me with favors. Among these was permission to walk each day in the park, although naturally in the company of my servant.

"But two of his favors were to have disastrous consequences for me and plague me for the rest of my life.

"The bey had a large supply of alcohol in the house. Drinking was a new thing for me, and unfortunately my tongue was agreeably tickled by sweet liqueurs. Under their ignoble influence my sad sense of reality was altered, and my head drifted into more pleasurable places. I found this state to my liking and wanted more and more to drink. The bey served me all I wanted and served himself as well. We often got drunk together. And when we did, we'd both run around on all fours on the carpets, howling like wild beasts. He, above all, was transformed. His face was no longer human, but animal-like, and one evening he tried get me to jam one of my toes into his mouth. Instead of complying, I picked up a fire iron and whacked him in the face. He remained calmly seated on the floor, licking his lips at the blood that ran into his mouth. I spat in his face. He licked that, too.

"But the day after these nights of debauchery was atrocious. My head was heavy with pain, my face pale, my heart trembling. I would stay in bed until noon, moaning and groaning. And since the morning light was impossible to bear, the bey held it back with heavy curtains. And once the room was lit by numerous candles and perfumed with myrrh, our crazy games began anew.

"One night, very late, when I was in the height of drunkenness, four young girls burst into the smoking room. They had tambourines and castanets, and began seductively dancing. My heart began beating with excitement. They were four Kyras, dressed like princesses but with their faces lightly veiled.

"I got up, upset my coffee cup, my liqueur glass and my hookah, and fell at their feet. Stretched out on the floor in the middle of the room, my eyes closed, I felt for ever so long the bottom of their skirts caressing my face and their perfume wafting through the air and into my nostrils. And then I passed out.

"When I revived I was in my bed. But I couldn't believe my eyes or my senses and could not at first take in the odious reality in front of me. Four revolting prostitutes—old, wrinkled, hideously naked—were caressing me, kissing me, teasing me in all ways, and covering my face and body with their slather. I tried to push them off and cried out for help. They pushed back tenderly. I finally freed myself from their arms, and picking up a set of fire tongs I began smashing everything in the room: mirrors, vases, statues, knick-knacks, anything that came within my reach.

"Startled, the disgusting whores ran out of the room, and went to report to Mustafa bey that I had refused to recognize them as the four beautiful girls of a few hours before.

"After this orgy, I shut myself up in my room for twenty-four hours and refused to see anyone. Since food made me nauseous, I gave it all to Wolf, and confessed to him how low I'd fallen.

"Finally, completely disgusted by the abject life forced on me by the bey, I decided to hang myself. I asked to see my master so as to tell him that if he did not consent to freeing me, I would put my plan to kill myself into action. But I was told that the bey was away for ten days. This unexpected news was totally surprising and immensely comforting. My head began to spin with new ideas of how I night escape.

"It was March. The day after the bey had left I took a walk in the park, escorted by my servant. Suddenly a question sprang into my mind: 'How did Wolf get in and out of the park?' The grounds were completely surrounded by old and very high walls, impossible to scale, and the large entry gate was always shut. There had to be an opening somewhere along the length of the bramble and ivy covered wall. I began discreetly examining the wall and finally noticed a place where the foliage was disturbed. I pretended to have an urgent need, left my vile servant on the path, and penetrated the bushes. As I suspected, I discovered at the base of the wall a place where it had recently fallen in, and as a result created a large passageway into the rarely traveled lands on the other side. I noted that the spot was directly opposite my windows.

"That same night, imprisoned in that fortress, my mind was on fire. Freedom was only two hundred feet from my room. But how could I get through the thick bars on my window that were fixed into solid oak window frames?

"Around midnight, my light out, I tried to rip the bars from their frame. When that proved impossible, I tried, with my jackknife, to cut the frame in order to free the bars. That was of no use either. I was maddened by my lack of success. Outside was a full moon, the tranquility of nature, space, freedom. Inside was captivity, debauchery, tyranny. I could see that once the bey returned, so too would return the nightly sessions with all their accompaniments. I felt myself being swallowed whole. My room seemed to be an infernal cage possessed by demons. A cold shiver ran up my spine, tears flooded my face, and my body began trembling so uncontrollably that I bit my tongue so violently it started bleeding.

"My watch said two o'clock in the morning. A sepulchral silence reigned throughout the house.

"In a frenzy I piled kindling and paper on the window sill, and set a match to it. I stood trembling, amazed at what I had done, as the flames began to devour the window frame. The room rapidly filled with smoke, and for a few moments I had to hold my jaw together with both hands to avoid crying out for help. I seized a fireplace hook, and with all my strength ripped out two bars, along with part of the burning frame. They landed in a hail of sparks on the floor, and continued to burn. I snatched up my money, leapt through the flaming window, and ran as fast as I could toward the wall.

"But mad excitement combined with the darkness conspired against me. I couldn't locate the breach in the wall at first, and in a panic I began to run backwards and forwards. I plunged into the brambles, cutting my face and hands. Finally, I saw the opening, and with a cry of joy I bounded through it, heedless of the blood streaming down my face!

"Two hours later, with the help of some beautiful gold pieces, I was on the Asiatic coast. From there, at daybreak, I looked toward Pera where giant tongues of flames were rising, vengefully to the sky. It was just one more fire in Constantinople, a city that was accustomed to being engulfed in flames.

"That evening a coach brought me to the door of an inn in a little Turkish village; two evenings later I slept in Smyrna, and eight days after that I smoked a very nice hookah on the terrace of a grand café in Beirut.

"But that's not the end…

"I now considered myself able to see life more clearly and was no longer easily duped. I was sixteen years old, and my wealth of past experiences had resulted in my dividing society into three kinds of people. In the first category were sweet and loving people like Kyra and my mother. The second type was made up of brutes like my father, and in the third group were others, like Mustafa bey, whose kindness had to be guarded against.

"As I sat on the terrace I was careful not to get too close to two chess players who appeared friendly. I thought of my poor Wolf, who took so long to accept my petting him, and I did as he had done. I resisted, at every turn, giving into being petted by strange hands that wanted to caress my young cheeks.

"But unfortunately I was so on guard against these types that I didn't even realize that I was about to fall into another ditch. Not everyone, I came to find out, fell into one of my three categories.

"I had rented a room above the beautiful terrace of the Great Variety Concert Hall, in the only public square in Beirut. The café was crowded from morning to night with highly cosmopolitan patrons. I was not drawn to the elegant folks who gathered there. Instead, I found far more charming the troupe of entertainers who performed in the variety show at the theater. Men and women, old and young, beautiful and ugly, they all lived life to the fullest. They quickly sized up everyone in the place, and always had a few words to exchange with the patrons who were not part of their company. As I was one of the habitués, they also said a few words to me as well. And to my delight, they sized me up as someone whom they could accept.

"These entertainers were Italian, Greek and French. They stayed in the same hotel as I. A young Greek couple, who sang quite well, lived across the narrow corridor from my room. I didn't care for the man but the woman attracted me. She knew this, although I tried to be discreet in throwing looks at her. Alone and nearly naked, she would sit in her room. When I went out, I always found her door open. This embarrassed me terribly, and I would try to close my eyes but something stronger than my will made me open them.

"One day we met in the darkness of the hallway, and she put her arms around me, gave me a fiery kiss, and said, 'This young man is much too timid. He needs to be encouraged.'

"Dazed by this encounter, I said to myself as I sat in my room, 'Oh well. What harm can come from a woman kissing a young man?

"And I was still a young man. She had said so, herself. My clothes, my independence, my expensive drinks proved this. But I was not thinking well; indeed, I had lost my head. But who ever thinks well in situations like these?

"One afternoon I was looking out my window at the crowds gathered in the square, and thinking about the playfulness, the voice and the allure of the actress. This caused me to remember, with great sadness, the extraordinary Kyra. Suddenly the door to my room opened, and the singer entered.

"I froze with fear.

"'My little one,' she said. 'There's nothing to be afraid of. He's downstairs totally absorbed in gambling.'

"She put her arms around my neck.

"I protested. "I don't want you to stay here.'

"I stayed close to her, on the bed, which I didn't find so hard to do.

"'What? You're chasing me out? You want me, who loves you, and who thinks you love me, to leave?'

"She spoke these words quite tenderly, all the while kissing me. I don't know how, but in the midst of caressing me, she opened the door and brought in a platter on which she had a bottle of imported wine and some cakes. I found them delicious. She had others brought. And I kept up with her in every way, partly out of bravado, enjoying the cakes and the wine and her. And her caresses! Her kisses!

"But I felt she was going farther with me than I would have liked, and I blushed.

"'You know, my darling,' she said. 'You're not good at anything! And at your age!'

"To put me at ease, she asked, 'Are you a Turkish subject?'

"'I don't know.'

"'What do your papers say?'

"'I don't have any papers.'

"'What? You are travelling in Turkey without papers? That's very stupid, my friend. You could be arrested!'

"I was terrified. I wouldn't have been able to do anything had someone told me that Mustafa bey had sent the police to my door.

"I begged her not to inform on me. And she promised to protect me. Again, I had a protector! What a travesty! Wasn't there some way, any way, to live without protection? Black thoughts seized me again. She began stroking my fingers.

"'You have such beautiful rings! Don't you want to give me one?'

"I felt I couldn't refuse my protector's request.

"My life was ruined. I hadn't even had two weeks of freedom. An invisible hand was stretching from Constantinople to Beirut, menacing me again. But a very visible hand and a much closer one presented me with a bill for the cakes and wine which cost more than my month's rent. In paying this bill, I thought, 'Between this extortion and my ring, I don't have much freedom left.'

"A few days later I realized how true this was.

"The singer and her husband were constantly present, practically to the point where they had taken over my room. One day, during a backgammon game, a policeman came up to me and said, 'Do you live here, sir?'

"'Yes, sir, I do," I said, as I tried to stifle my fear.

"'Very well, then. Please come to the police station tomorrow morning so that we can review your papers.'

"He graciously nodded goodbye to my companions and left. I was frozen in fear.

"'Don't do it!' cried my protector. 'My husband will go right away to tell Mamour to leave you alone. They're friends.'

"I thanked them effusively.

"In reality, I was not bothered again by the police. Very aware of this, I even began to think of other ways to prove my gratitude to my friends other than offering them meals. The solution arrived quite quickly.

"'I've not had any luck gambling today, my friend,' the husband said to me without hesitation. 'Would you lend me two Turkish pounds?'

"'Of course,' I replied.

"His bad luck continued, and he came the next day to ask for two more pounds. And the next day again, he asked for money. By the end of the week his continuous losing streak made me think that if this continued, I'd be out of money within three months. That same evening without thinking too much about it, I took the road to Damascus in the company of two fat rug dealers.

"As I bounced about in their *araba* I mulled over the complexity of life. 'Now,' I said to myself, 'I need to be on guard against women who kiss men in dark hallways.'

"Just as Saint Paul was blinded on the road to Damascus, my life, too, changed on that very same road.

"Damascus first struck me as a city upon which God had liberally sprinkled dust from the four corners of the world. When I got out of the *araba* I felt much lighter in my spirit.

"I had dressed as a poor Greek in order not to attract attention. My belongings were tied up in a big handkerchief which I carried under my arm. I had secured my *kemir,* or money belt, in which I had placed my money and jewels, under my clothes. Disguised in this way, I felt myself free from 'protectors' that I did not need. In the Cadem district I looked for a cheap inn along the narrow streets that were more like tunnels, as they were flanked by tall buildings on both sides. At one inn the Greek proprietor told me that to get a room as cheap as I wanted, I would have to share with someone else. I accepted, and he took me to see the room where I could put down my bindle. I asked him who occupied the other bed.

"'A man like you,' he said sharply.

"I got a lump in my throat. My country, Kyra, and mama were en-shrouded in a long shadow that I could not reach; and what was I, who had never been so far away from them, to do now? What would I find in this sinister city? How would I ever find my sister? And how would I make a living once I had spent all my money? Not only that, I didn't have papers. This was another serious worry. Would I be arrested and thrown into jail?

"In the courtyard of the inn, around a fountain surrounded by flower beds, some people were sitting Turkish style, smoking, and drinking milk mixed with spirits. They seemed to be enjoying themselves. They were at home here, knew each other, helped one another, shared joys and sorrows. What was I to them? A stranger. Would any of them venture into the room of a stranger who was dying from sadness to ask if they could do something to help?

"Instinctively, I placed my hand on my *kemir* where I had stashed my money. This was my only friend! But gold is a friend that treacherously takes leave without regret, and I knew of no way to make it stay. Kyra was totally different! She wouldn't have left me for anything in the world. We were inseparable. Would there be another Kyra in all the world? Maybe. But every city and town had its Dragomir, and for them, I was a stranger who passed by, perhaps out of curiosity, worthy of looking at for a brief moment and then forgetting.

"To console myself, I ordered a brandy, then another. The dinner hour arrived. I ordered a light meal and a glass of wine, then another. And with a heart heavy with worries, I went up to my room.

"In my room a man of about thirty, half dressed, was sitting on the edge of his bed. A little gas lamp burned on the table. Two chairs. Two questionably clean beds. A smoky mirror. No sink.

"I said 'good evening' in Greek, and looked at my bed.

"'Keep your bed away from the wall,' he told me, as if we were old friends. 'There are bugs. And we have to keep the lamp lit all night; bugs, like owls, are afraid of light.'

"'What bugs?' I asked, as I knew nothing about them. What was he talking about?

"'You don't know about bugs? Oh well, you'll find out tonight. But tell me, where have you been sleeping before tonight where you did not make their acquaintance? I've never known a bed that didn't have bugs.'

"'Do they bite?' I asked, afraid now of this new enemy.

"'A little,' he said, rather indifferently.

"I wanted to get undressed and get into bed as I was quite tired, but I was seized by shyness about doing it in front of a stranger. He understood and turned down the lamp. When I had slipped under the covers, he turned it up again.

"'You act like a girl,' he said laughing.

"His humor made me feel much better. I slept well that night, with my *kemir* under my pillow.

"The next morning I had no more knowledge of bugs than I had had the night before. But my companion pointed out a little spot of blood on the pillow. Almost happy, I boldly got dressed in front of him.

"A burst of voices and loud laughter filtered in from the courtyard. I looked out the window and saw a group of men around the fountain, smoking their large Turkish *cubuk* pipes, and drinking coffee. I breathed in the fresh air, letting it fill my lungs. A yellow light, mysterious and oriental, floated over the courtyard.

"I got ready to go out but the tender enemy who lived in my heart made me ask the stranger, 'Would you like to join me for coffee?'

"Downstairs, we talked while smoking pipe after pipe. He told me his troubles. He was without work or money and in debt. I then told him that I had a problem, too.

"'I've lost my papers,' I said. 'If you know how I can get new ones, I'll give you a Turkish pound as a reward.'

"He lit his pipe. 'Yes, I can arrange that,' he said in a low voice. 'There's a public scribe here who can get them. But he'll ask for plenty of money.'

"'How much?' I asked him, quite pleased.

"'Four Turkish pounds.'

"'I'll pay that much, and give you the pound I promised, as well.'

"An hour later a scribe with a long white beard swore before a government functionary that I had been born in Stamboul on a certain year of the Hegira, that I was therefore a Turkish subject, loyal to the Sultan, our master, and that my name was Stavro.

"The bureaucrat listened, smiling. Then taking out a feather pen, he covered a long paper with beautiful Arabic script, signed it, had the old man sign it, and applied the imperial seal. He then offered me this precious talisman.

"'You need to offer him a little bribe,' the scribe whispered.

"I put a pound on the table.

"'That's not enough,' the old man said.

"I went to a corner of the room and rummaged around again in my *kemir*, then returned and put down another. Outside I paid off the scribe for his false testimony. Then, with my companion, we set off to see the town, eating and drinking along the way.

"When we returned that evening we were both drunk and happy and fell into our beds. I slept deeply forgetting about the bugs but not neglecting to put my *kemir* safely under my head.

"Upon waking I was astonished to find myself alone in my room. But I was astonished even more to realize that my *kemir* had vanished along with my traitorous and heartless roommate. All I had left were a few little coins and that ill-gotten talisman.

"There was no point in crying. Now I was going to die.

"I have never forgotten the pain that gripped my stomach, the emptiness in my chest. I thought my life was over.

"In my underwear I whirled around the room, and without knowing why, I leaned out the window. In the courtyard as usual, the same people sat around the fountain, smoking. They seemed to me like gravediggers guarding a grave. And then I jumped into the void. The next thing I knew was that blood was streaming down my face and I was suffocating. When the innkeeper and my fellow residents arrived I could only say:

"'The... *kemir.*'

"They all began questioning me at once wanting to know everything. But I couldn't say anything else except 'the *kemir.*'

"'What about your *kemir?*'

"'The... *kemir.*'

"They poured water over my head, washed the blood off my face, and forced me to drink some spirits.

"'Speak,' said the innkeeper, shaking me by my lapels.

"'The... *kemir,*' I said over and over again.

"'I understand,' said the innkeeper. The guy who slept in the other bed must have stolen his *kemir* as a way of thanking him for last night's revels!'

"All I wanted to do was stand up and walk away but he made me stay seated on a chair. I was in agony, and waved my arms about madly.

"'Yes, this is awful. Somebody stole your coins. But you can't kill yourself because of this. You're not the only one this has happened to. How many *chereks* did you have?'

"'The... *kemir*,' I said again.

"'What? This boy doesn't know how to say anything except 'The... *kemir*.'

"After saying this the innkeeper went up to my room and returned with my clothes.

"'Come on, get dressed!' he said.

"I was frozen in place as if I were paralyzed, and so the innkeeper had to dress me from head to toe. Afterward, he dug in my pockets, pulled out my identity papers and a few coins."

"'Look here,' he cried. 'You're not so poor as all that. You've got three *medjidies*. And your name is Stavro. Three *medjidies* will keep you from dying of hunger. What sort of work can you do?'

"'The *kemir*.'

"'Oh, you and your blasted *kemir*!' he yelled. He put everything back in my pockets and began walking away. Then, over his shoulder he cried: 'Anyway, you didn't have enough in that *kemir* to buy a camel, because if you had, you wouldn't have been staying at my place!'

"I had enough in my *kemir* to buy far more than just a camel. I had eight-three Turkish gold pieces, nine rings with precious stones, and a watch. And with that fortune, yes, I came to stay at his inn.

"It is not true at all that human beings are creatures who understand life. Their intelligence doesn't serve them terribly well; just because they can talk doesn't make them su p erior to animals. Indeed, they are actually stupider than animals when it comes to being able to guess and understand the suffering of their fellow beings.

"From time to time we see in the streets a man with a ghastly pale face clearly unable to find his way, or a woman weeping. If we were truly superior beings, we would stop that man or that woman and immediately offer them assistance. All this about man being superior to beasts is utterly false.

"I don't remember that well—it's been more than fifty years—how I got out of my chair in the courtyard of the inn, and how, as confused as I was, I managed to cross the city from one side to another. But I do know that not one hand reached out to that young man who wandered along like an automaton with glazed eyes. Not one voice called out to me, not one human face even took any notice of me at all. In a dazed state, on a beautiful April afternoon, I arrived somehow at Baptouma Promenade.

"I was jolted back into reality by a series of oaths directed at me by a raging Arab coach driver who nearly knocked me over. I felt for my belt, where my *kemir* had been. My heart beat like a bird held in one's hand, while a lump all the way from my stomach rose to my throat cutting off my breath. Each time I put my hand on my belt my heart began fluttering again, shortening my breath. I needed terribly to convince myself that it was actually true, that I had been a thief's victim, that I no longer had my *kemir*. In moments of great distress sensitive hearts often find it difficult to accept the idea that something terrible has happened to them and that they can't do anything about it.

"People out for a stroll passed me on each side. Happy couples, women with babies, fat gentlemen content with themselves all looked at me as they walked by but saw nothing, understood nothing. And I felt I was dying. I alone had to bear the unbearable that was too much for my youth, my soul, my inexperience of making my way in the world.

"I kept on walking and finally came to the Syrian countryside with its muddy roads and Bedouin tents. Life seemed to be absent, especially in my own empty self. Whenever I began to look at something, my hand instinctively went to my belt, and my mind repeated, 'you don't any longer have your *kemir.*' And again, I would feel nearly asphyxiated.

"An Arab child, riding on a donkey, passed slowly near me. He was leading a camel that carried two large packs that shifted from side to side with each step. The ugliness of this creature with eyes like a snake frightened me. A little farther along, a Bedouin with a wild black beard and copper-colored skin came galloping up on a horse. He stopped and asked me a question in Arabic. But I couldn't respond. He took off, leaving me disquieted, for he made me recall the beautiful head of my Uncle Cosma.

"A little while later I came to a village of rudimentary houses, where some barefoot men, sitting on the ground were turning wood, using both hands and feet. The women, their faces veiled, looked like scarecrows in their tattered and dirty black garments. They carried water jugs on their heads while their filthy and undernourished children played and screamed like little devils. A man was removing hot flat round bread from a mud oven dug into the earth. The aroma of fresh dough drifted over to me.

"I wanted to get through the village in haste but I noticed that a docile dog was following on my heels. I stopped. He stopped. We looked each other right in the eyes. He was dark gray, about the size of Wolf, but the poor thing didn't have a shred of dignity nor Wolf's sense of independence nor calm composure. He lowered his head humbly, crouching in fear. His eyes expressed uncertainty, humility and worry. I felt sorry for him and patted his head. He licked my hand. He was not hard to please.

"I went back to the oven and bought for two *meteliks* four pieces of bread. He ate them all and I bought some more, put them in my pockets, and started off again. He followed as before.

"A sand dune, barren of any vegetation, rose up in front of me. I climbed it quickly, but by the time I reached the top I was out of breath and sat down next to the dog. Before my eyes Damascus, studded with cupolas and minarets, stretched out far and wide like an immense cemetery covered in white dust.

"I couldn't hear a thing except the sound of my dying heart beating violently within me. I closed my eyes, and Damascus and the world disappeared. What sprang up was the past, and I relived those wonderful days in my mother's house. The sweet existence of those years, so far off now, insinuated itself under my closed eyelids. I lived again all those joyous years, recalled every intimate detail of my life from my earliest memories to the terrible night of the murder, and finally our abduction.

"Suddenly it leaped into my mind that the evil that had befallen both Kyra and me was the result of having provoked that crime and acted as accomplices. Our suffering was penance for our deeds. We had wished for the death of our father and brother, and this could only be a mortal sin. Now God was punishing us, Kyra and me, she with slavery and I with disastrous freedom.

"I opened my eyes and was startled. The sky was blood red. Low clouds, like clots of blood, hovering and slowly moving just above the ground, were taking on all sorts of fantastic shapes, one more frightful than the other.

"In front of the little grotto where I was curled up, I lay down, my face to the ground, my eyes covered with my hands and asked forgiveness from God, from my father, and from the soul of my murdered brother.

"When night fell it wrapped in its darkness the body of a repentant adolescent who sought consolation in the misery of a dog sent to him by chance.

"Prayers and penance are supposed to soothe the souls of believers, and I passed several hours quite pleasantly. But the approach of dawn, in the desert, brings with it terrible cold. When the sun came up over the horizon of the Levant, I was shivering, and I thought I might have caught a chill that would cost me my life. I said to myself, 'If I die having repented, God will pardon me. My soul will not be damned to eternal hell.'

"I got up and took the road back to the village. I ate some bread on the route; the three other pieces I gave to the dog, who was even more famished than I.

"In a little while the sun began to warm my back and I started to feel a kindly peace welling up in me. I arrived in the village, which now seemed to me less ugly. There the dog decided to go its own way. This caused me to feel a little sad, but I patted his head and I left him as one would leave someone he had met on a short trip.

"Alone, now, still tight in the throat from having had my *kemir* stolen, I took the road through the forest that led to Baptouma and Damascus. A long camel caravan crossed the road without my being afraid of them. I reentered the streets of Baptouma a little before noon. The weather was splendid, and I was astonished by how much activity there was. The streets were crowded by carriages and people on foot. Going here and there were men in beautiful Turkish garb, and young beautiful women, most of them with their faces covered by only a light white veil. I could hear all around me sonorous voices, bursts of laughter like the clinking of crystal glasses tapped by a baton, and animated conversations. I was overwhelmed by the charm of the voices and the delightful clothes. It was then I remembered that today was Friday, that is, Sunday for Moslems. The greetings between the women were refined, gracious and discreet. The men, however, were far more effusive with their '*Asalaam 'Alaykums*' and their repeated handshakes. Occasionally their extended greetings caused the pedestrian flow to come to an abrupt halt. A fair amount of Turkish was spoken, but Arabic dominated the exchanges.

"I watched the procession for some time, enthralled with the comings and goings. Finally fewer carriages and pedestrians were to be seen. My heart was filled with contradictory emotions: the desire to live, the thirst for happiness, my misery, my bad luck. Pensive and troubled, I continued my rambles. I soon found myself alone and feeling sad. A beautiful carriage led by two fine horses trotted up beside me. Just as they were about to pass, I suddenly felt breathless and my heart stopped beating.

"Kyra was in the carriage!

"Yes, I still believe that it was my sweet sister, whom I so dearly loved, in that carriage! She was wearing the odalisque outfit in which Nazim Effendi had dressed her, complete with veil, looking just like the paintings on the yacht's cabin wall.

"I reeled unsteadily, beat the air with my arms, and cried out in Romanian,'Kyra! Kyralina! It's me. Dragomir!'

"The young woman smiled through her transparent veil and waved her gloved hand at me, but the coachman snapped his whip. The eunuch who sat next to him glared coldly at me, and the horses picked up speed.

"I thought I was going to die. Yes, it was Kyra; she had waved at me! I set off as fleet as an ostrich after the carriage, saying to myself, 'All powerful Lord! Just hours after I confessed my sin to You and repented, You have already bestowed Your grace upon me by giving me back my lost sister!'

"The carriage, despite my rapid pace, got away from me. I struggled on, out of breath, thinking it was gone from me forever. Then to my utter delight, I saw it emerging from a wood and drive up to a splendid villa. The huge gate opened slowly, swallowed up the carriage, and then closed behind it.

"I cried out with joy. With all my waning strength I threw myself against the gates, beating it with my fists and feet. A few minutes later a little door opened on the side of the large gates, and a man in uniform appeared.

"'Kyra!' I screamed. And then catching my breath I added, in Turkish, 'she's my sister. I have to speak to her.'

"'What? What do you want?' said the guard, also in Turkish. And he put out his hand to stop me from entering.

"'The lady in the carriage. That's...that's my sister...Kyra.'

"'What Kyra? Are you mad?'

"I was, of course, mad. I pushed aside the guard, slipped around him and managed to get into the courtyard. But I didn't get farther than that. Two men grabbed me, and from a window came the shout of an old man:

"'What's this disturbance all about? Take this *gâvur*—this Christian—and flog him some, as well as the guard who let him in.'

"I was led out of the courtyard, thrown on the ground, and whipped with a bull's pizzle that ripped open my trousers and buttocks. Then my torturers bolted the gates, leaving me half-conscious from pain.

"This was the culmination of my suffering, the end of the continual torment that I had endured for more than three years. Though God was cruel in His refusal to reunite me with Kyra, He still blessed me. His blessing was sending me a friend.

"I pulled together what little strength I had in my half-dead body and staggered to the other side of the street. There, I fell to the ground, exhausted. At this moment a man, somewhere between forty and forty-five, walked over to me. He was poorly dressed in old Greek-style clothing and carried in one hand a salep *ibrik* and in the other a basket with cups and utensils. He put these down on the ground, and crossing his arms, exclaimed sympathetically in Greek, 'Oh, my poor boy. I saw you get flogged, but I was powerless to help you! What did you do to make those heathen so mistreat you?'

"I looked at his face, imprinted with sincerity, his unkempt and graying beard, his kind eyes and wrinkled brow. And despite myself, in a fit of rage, I yelled, 'Go to hell! Leave me in peace!'

"And then I broke into sobs.

"He was undeterred. 'Why do you want me to go to hell, my child? I truly pity you and want to help you.'

"'Leave me alone,' I moaned. 'I've had enough of men like you with pity in their hearts. Let me die alone!'

"'Oh, how awful! So young, and already disgusted with life. But still, have this cup of warm salep. It will make you feel a little better.'

"I accepted his cup of warm salep, but didn't know what to think. What understanding could I draw from my short experience of life except that men who begin by seeming good and kind and generous, in the end turn out to be perverts and criminals. Even though I was only sixteen, I knew quite well to what depths human beings can descend. But I didn't know everything.

"I didn't know that God made His creatures infinitely complex and varied, that suffering a thousand setbacks does not give one the right to dismiss all of humanity. God, Himself, knew this when angry with His sinful creations, He decided to punish them without killing them all. Indeed, He saved a just patriarch and his family. It is true that those who came after the flood were not worth more than their predecessors, but that wasn't His fault. It's that God (like me at sixteen) didn't know the world all that well and didn't know what people were capable of doing.

"I do know that since the day when destiny sent me Barba Yani, salep seller and divine soul, I could consider myself happy. He who has the opportunity to encounter in his life a Barba Yani will be a blessed man. He's unique among those I've known. He helped me to meet life head on, and frequently I stop to bless him and sing his praises. The goodness of one man is more powerful than the wickedness of a thousand. Evil dies with the evil; goodness continues to live on long after the good are gone. As the sun that disperses the clouds and returns joy to the earth, Barba Yani replaced the sickness in my soul with health. This did not happen without resistance on my part; I strongly opposed his efforts. But whose heart, even one as tortured by life as mine had been, could have ultimately repelled his extraordinary goodness?

"I yielded to him, and that saintly salep seller understood all about what had happened to me. His remedy was as rapid as a lightning bolt, 'Stavraki!' he said, wisely using the diminutive of my adopted name, 'you must, right now, give up looking for your sister in such an unwise way. To free a woman shut up in a harem is as easy as snatching a deer from the jaws of a tiger. If you can get this nonsense out of your head and heart, everything else will be as easy as greeting the morning. You've got three *medjidies* in your pocket. That's enough to buy a salep *ibrik* and cups like what you see in my hands and that has allowed me to live freely for twenty years. And then, with the brass *ibrik* in one hand and the basket full of cups in the other, and with Barba Yani next to you, we'll go gaily through the streets to the squares, to the festivals, to the fairs, crying out joyously 'Salep! Salep! Salep! Here come the *salepci!* The good land of the Levant will open freely and far and wide for you, a free man. Whatever they say about Turkish tyranny, there is no place else where you can live as freely. But on one condition: you must efface yourself, disappear among the masses, not invite notice, be deaf and dumb. Then, and only then, can you go anywhere, invisible. Shut doors don't open by forcing them.

"Not later than the next day, my arms loaded with my *ibrik* and my basket of cups, I cried out spiritedly, alongside Barba Yani, 'Salep! Salep!' And I saw now how to live without my *kemir,* that traitorous friend, and without hardening my heart. The coins fell from all sides, freedom entered my purse, and as night fell I savored the sense of well being that can come to a man without having his pockets full of gold. As we smoked our hookahs on a terrace, I soaked up the kindness and good will that radiated from Barba Yani. I loved him the way one loves a good father or a friend. I stayed with him, worked with him, and ate with him. We spent our free time together. In short, we were inseparable. A strong friendship quickly developed between us, and I felt as if I, a young branch, had been grafted onto the trunk of a great tree. Barba Yani met my curiosity about him even before I asked, and recounted his life to me. He had not lived so perfectly in the past and had had his share of misfortune.

"He had been a *daskalos,* or school teacher in a little village in Greece. He had committed a crime of passion that got him two years in prison and stripped him of his license to teach. Upon getting out of prison, he had to leave the town. He wandered to a good many others, worked as a merchant, had his ups and downs, made friends, and allowed his heart to bleed for others. Another amorous adventure almost cost him his life. After that he went to Turkey and lived alone, independently, and mostly wisely.

"He was a man who knew how to talk and how to keep his silence. He gave of his good will without becoming foolish, and once he had made a decision to do something, he could not be persuaded to take a different course. He knew all the dialects of the Near East and he spent his free time reading, taking walks and washing his linen. He never insisted I do something but always showed me the best, most useful and smartest way to proceed. Thanks to him I learned to read and write

Greek. He could see I was faithfully attached to him, and he was not stingy in his affection for me. At the beginning he was 'Mister Yani' for me, but he asked me to call him 'Barba,' or uncle in Greek. In becoming his disciple, friend, and the comfort of his old age, I forgot about the loss of my *kemir* with its precious treasure. But before that, I still had a tall hill to climb. But we climbed it together.

"While it was true that I had forgotten about the theft of my *kemir,* I couldn't let go of Kyra. I loved Barba Yani but I adored Kyra. I was certain that she was residing behind the door of that villa where I had been whipped, and some inner demon kept prodding me to go back there.

"It was the middle of summer, three months after I had spied Kyra in the carriage. I made a number of visits alone to that evil fortress without telling Barba Yani. I would walk around from some distance away, reconnoitering, always on the lookout for some sign of Kyra. Other women came and went in the carriage but never Kyra.

"Encouraged by how undetected I had been in my attempts to spy on the villa, I decided one very dark night to become a bit bolder. I got a ladder and leaned it against the high wall of the courtyard. What I wanted to do was see inside the harem where I knew the women would not be wearing veils. But I found all of the blinds drawn. I didn't give up, however, but continued along the wall until finally I found one window open to the night air. Through the window I could see a large room, richly furnished, but no one was in sight. I waited at the top of the ladder, my heart beating, hoping that some women would soon appear in the room.

"Suddenly the rung on which I was standing cracked loudly, and I almost fell. Frozen with fear, I hung on as well as I could. But then the ladder began shaking violently, and a moment later I could feel it being pulled away from the wall. I fell into the arms of a guard who, without saying a word, began beating me with his fists. I was then tied up, shoved into a donkey cart and taken immediately to Damascus where I was thrown into prison.

"Ottoman prisons during that time were true dungeons. The poor souls who were locked up there, especially for a crime as serious as mine, never knew how long it would be before a judge would hear their case unless someone with some influence and the right number of gifts implored the potentate to move things along. The loss of liberty, of course, was awful, but that was nothing compared to the horrors one had to endure inside, particularly if one were a young man. There were a dozen inmates in my cell. We had one bed between us—if you can call some bare boards a bed—that took up three quarters of the cell. A large wooden tub with a cover that was supposed to serve as a toilet occupied one corner of the room. The odor it discharged was nearly asphyxiating. Head and body lice were rampant as were the regiments of rats that came and went at will. We didn't even try to kill them; they were owed life as much as anyone.

"The most disgusting practices went on in front of everyone's eyes. Neither Turks, Greeks, Armenians nor Arabs were human any longer. But it would be wrong to say that they had become animals, for no animal is capable of falling to such degrading and disgusting depths.

"It was into this earthly hell, into this realm of monsters, that I fell. For them, my arrival was a tremendous gift. No one came to my defense, no one protected me, neither Muslims nor Christians. Instead, they fought over the fresh meat, pulled each other's beards, bloodied one another. Had they been armed, they would have killed each other. For a month I was their prey, suffering the most atrocious violations that one could even imagine. Or not imagine!

"Today, I don't regret the month I spent in hell for I saw how base human beings could become, how low they could descend. If I have any good left in me after all I've seen and all I've suffered, I use it simply to pay homage to Him who created all goodness. Though rarely, He gave it freely, even distributing it in the midst of brutes, allowing life to be lived in the most abject circumstances.

"I felt as if I had been buried alive and thought a great deal about death. I had heard that prisoners who could no longer bear the constant tortures hanged themselves from the window bars using strips of cloth torn from their clothing. I decided to emulate those martyrs one night while everyone was asleep.

"But a voice inside me continued to whisper hope. I knew that I was not alone in the world as before. One man with a huge heart, an extraordinary and rare friend, was outside. He was poor and without protectors, but he was good and he was smart. He would be thinking of me, working somehow to regain my freedom.

"I was right. One day the door of the cell opened, the warden entered, and behind him, Barba Yani. Only the sight of Kyra could have made me as happy. But at the same time, I felt sad because my friend's hair had turned white from worrying about me. I threw myself into his arms and sobbed into his chest. A Greek on the bed, rather than being moved by this painful scene of reunion, cried out, 'Hey, old man, is that your boy? He's fancy goods for this place, and we've treated ourselves. Are you the one who got the best of him?'

"Barba Yani went as white as a winding sheet. He held me in his arms, and said in a choking and trembling voice, 'Be strong! Be strong! Tomorrow you'll get out of here. They're going to deport you from Damascus!'

"'Deport me?' I cried. 'But I'll be sent away from you.'

"'It was the softest penalty I could get. Your offense was serious. You tried, at night, to sneak into a harem. Anyway, don't worry. I'm going along with you. The world is large, we will be free, and if you listen to me from now on, you'll be happy, even on Turkish soil. I've got to say goodbye now. Be ready tomorrow at dawn.'

"I couldn't sleep at all that night. At dawn, two policemen on horseback, with rifles and sabers came to the door of my cell to get me. When I got outside I saw that they had a cart in which two other men were already seated. Barba Yani was also there with the other two deportees, and he had brought all of our belongings. The convoy took off on the road to Diarbekir.

"It's not easy to tell or write down the life story of a man. To narrate the life of a man who has loved the world and journeyed through it is even more difficult. But when that man is full of passion and has known the heights of happiness and the depths of misery in traveling through that world, to give a vivid account of his life is almost impossible. It's also not easy for those who want to hear the tale.

"What is charming, picturesque or interesting about the tumultuous life and adventures of a man with a fierce soul is not always found in the more prominent facts of his life. Beauty resides far more frequently in the details. But who wants to hear details? Who can take pleasure in those seeming trifles of existence? Above all, who can understand what they mean? That is why I have always turned down requests to 'tell the story of your life!'

"There is another problem as well. When one is in love, one does not live alone. One doesn't even live alone if he doesn't want to be loved as is the case with me today. Those who have passion in their hearts never cease to live on memories, for there is no memory, no past, without a present. It's beautiful to want to die. And I have sincerely wished for that several times in my life. But the lovely faces from my past that live within me have softened my heart, have replaced grief with joy, and have caused me again and again to seek life among other like-minded spirits. One of those beautiful figures was Barba Yani.

"I can't say anything, or much of anything, about him. For eight years my life was joined to his. Our shadows darkened Diarbekir, Aleppo, Angora, Sivas, Erzerum and hundreds of other little cities and villages. And we sold more than just salep. Just about everything passed through our hands: carpets, handkerchiefs, cutlery, balms, drugs, perfume, horses, dogs and cats. But it was always salep that kept us from starving. Whenever some bad deal laid us low, we quickly got out our *ibriks,* those poor rusty *ibriks,* and resumed our old song, 'Salep! Salep! Here come the *salepcis!'*

"We laughed, yes, because Barba Yani was an incomparable friend. I, the incomparable screw-up, was the one who always brought on our disasters. Among my many screw-ups is one I remember well.

"We had used all of our money to buy two beautiful horses at a big fair outside of Angora. We were pleased because we'd gotten a good deal. On the fifteen kilometers back to Angora, partly because I was so happy and partly because I was so tired, I insisted we stop at a little isolated tavern. It was night, and Barba Yani was opposed to the idea.

"'Stavraki, let's keep going. We'll get something to drink when we get home.'

"'No, Barba Yani, here. Let's just stop for a minute. We need to honor our good luck.'

"The poor man gave in. We tied up the horses to a post outside. With our eyes at the window, we had our first glass of wine. Then another. We shoved down some food, and ordered carafe after carafe. Barba Yani loved a good time as much as I did, and soon we were singing,

'Once again you've gotten soused
Once again you're smashing glasses
Oh, what a wretched beast you've become'

"Suddenly, in the middle of the song, Barba Yani stopped singing. Calmly, he looked out the window, and said, 'Yes, Stavraki, you are a wretched beast. The beautiful beasts that were outside are gone, or else I can't see.'

"I was out of my chair and out the door in one motion only to hear the sound of galloping hooves resonating in the night air.

"An hour later, we were staggering along the dark road, falling into holes here and there. Barba Yani turned to me and said, 'You wanted to honor our good luck! Fine. Here we are now struggling along on foot, you stupid pup. To console yourself, sing for me 'Once Again You've Gotten Soused!'

"It's so good to feel your heart beating on the good human earth, on that earth that transmits to you its affirmation of life. It's perilous to ignore such bounty!

"Over the years in which my life was transformed by being with Barba Yani even the natural world became welcoming, poetic and fraternal. Everything appeared beautiful to me and worthy of living. Ugliness was no longer repelling; we dispelled foolishness with a good joke; we unmasked trickery, and I even came to understand how to live with oppression. When the world's vulgarity was about to suffocate us, we retreated into silence. There only the beauties of nature spoke to our eyes and hearts.

"Barba Yani could go a whole day without saying a word. With his eyes only he would show me what was worth looking at. He called this practice 'taking a cleansing bath,' and that's just what it was. The mute works of creation purify a man humiliated by the baseness of existence. And there's not a man, no matter how strong, who hasn't on his life's journey been infected by vileness.

"This great companion of my youth was also a repository of knowledge about the ancient world and its philosophers. All his pronouncements about life were illustrated with examples drawn from ancient wisdom. He himself was not a sage, but he loved clarity of mind and heart.

"'Sooner or later, an intelligent man will come to realize that the sentimental uproar that troubles the world and burns up life is simply inane,' he told me one day. 'Happy is he who realizes this early on, for he'll have a much better life.'

"One cold autumn day we found ourselves in a field near Aleppo where soldiers were on maneuver. We were overwhelmed with demand for our hot drinks. The officers even came to treat themselves, and as we had charcoal fires under our *ibriks,* they remained a while to warm themselves and talk with us. A commanding officer told his subaltern an anecdote about a general of Alexander the Great who wanted to accept Darius' offer of peace.

"'I would accept if I were Alexander, said the general. To which the great conqueror replied: I would accept if I were...if I were'

"The Turkish officer became confused.

"'Ah, what was the name of Alexander's friend?'

"'Parmenio,' said Barba Yani, who had been listening to the conversation.

"'Bravo, old man,' exclaimed the officer. 'How did you know that? One doesn't encounter Alexander the Great while selling salep.'

"'On the contrary. Everybody needs something to warm himself as you can see!'

"This pleased the officer, and he sat down to talk with us. I looked at him; he looked at me.

"'I've seen you somewhere before,' he said to me. 'You look familiar.'

"'You're right,' I said, blushing. We were in the same carriage with Mustafa bey five years ago in Constantinople.'

"'By Allah, that's true. You are the boy who was looking for his mother who had had her eye put out. You poor kid, you must have had quite a time with that damn satyr.'

"'More than that. But I didn't know who he was then.'

"'But how could you have put any faith in the first stranger who patted your cheeks?'

"The officer stayed a long while, and we talked and talked. He revealed to me further facts about the darker side of Mustafa bey. He also talked with Barba Yani, intrigued by his vast wisdom. When he left he put into each of our hands a Turkish pound.

"'It's not a tip,' he said. 'It's for the esteem I accord the wisdom of the old man and for the suffering of the young one.'

"When we got back home Barba Yani said, 'Do you see, Stavro? People are misled everywhere, but intelligence will break down all barriers even when one wears a uniform.'

"Barba Yani was aging, and his heart was making it more difficult each year for him to make a living. He would become tired quickly, and bouts of depression occurred more frequently. I was twenty-two by that time, strong, courageous and resourceful. I decided, since we'd saved up a little money, to convince Barba Yani to take a rest. To make our holiday even more pleasant, I chose to go to Mt. Lebanon since we had never been there.

"Oh beautiful and sad Mt. Lebanon! All I have to do is think of our year's stay there and my heart leaps and bleeds at the same time. Ghazir! Ghazir! And you, Dlepta! And you Harmon! And you Malmetein! And you, cedars that would love to hug the whole world with your long branches. And you, pomegranate trees, that need only three handfuls of moss in a rock's crevice to grow your delicious fruit you so kindly offer to travelers. And you, Mediterranean Sea, who gives yourself over to the caresses of your sun god. To all of you, I say goodbye. I will never see you again, but my eyes will always remember your unique and soft light. Life did not want my joy to be complete. But, then when has life ever gratified us with complete joyfulness?

"On the way to the summit, we set ourselves up in Ghazir, a little village which was as picturesque as almost anywhere in Lebanon. We were the only lodgers in the house of Set Amra, an old arthritic woman, who lived by herself. She was a Christian like all Lebanese. As fellow Christians we were well received, even though we were Orthodox, and she a Catholic. And there's a story here. My life is rich in stories.

"I went about earning our living, and Barba Yani, who now walked with a cane, spent his days searching for pomegranates and killing little snakes. We learned that Set Amra, with whom we talked a lot while smoking our hookahs, had known sorrow in her own life. She was alone, and this loneliness was hard for her. Her only child, a young woman twenty-years-old, was in Venezuela. She had gone there with her father who, like many Lebanese, had traveled abroad to make his fortune. The father had died, and for the last year since that tragedy, she had not written much to her mother. Selina, the young woman, was not poor. She ran her own jewelry business but had little affection for her mother. She seemed, in fact, to have forgotten her mother, and Set Amra felt that she'd have to spend her remaining days on earth poor and lonely.

"We felt sorry for her and began to take our meals with her. She became like a sister and mother to us. We treated her with good cuts of broiled mutton and made sure her hookah was always full of tobacco. She praised the Lord for having sent us to her and wrote letters to Selina in which she extolled our presence. In her letters Selina expressed her gratitude to the two strangers. And the days went by quite happily.

"I wasn't earning much money, and our savings were shrinking before our eyes. Autumn came and with it Barba Yani caught a bad cold. A doctor from Beirut and some medicine cured him, but it ate up all our money.

"The winter was severe, among the worst ever in Lebanon. I could barely bring in enough to keep us from starving. We gave up eating meat; and three days a week we had only dry bread. We allowed ourselves only one hookah, and passed it from hand to hand, mouth to mouth. It was hard but we made it to March. It was then that a startling piece of news reached us: Selina announced she was leaving Venezuela and would be home in three or four weeks. We shouted for joy and went overboard in expressing our delight again and again.

"'Do you know what?' Set Amra mysteriously asked us one day. 'Stavro is a handsome young man. Surely Selina would find you so, and your generosity toward me would be more than repaid. What do you think, Stavro?'

"What could Stavro say? As usual, I lost my head. I lost it so thoroughly that Barba Yani noticed, and the three of us danced around the room in celebration of my upcoming marriage to a woman who knew nothing about it.

"Like a horse with blinders, I looked neither to left no right. I began to consider the house as my future property. I noticed that the flat gravel-covered roof leaked when it rained, so I decided to roll it the way the Lebanese did. The sight of me on the roof gave the neighbors some good laughs, particularly when the roller smashed into my heels and pitched me onto my face. Oh my God, I've done so many stupid things in my life!

"I even went so far one day to point out to Barba Yani that Set Amra's lips were still red and full.

"'Barba Yani, look at those lips. What do you think? They might still know how to kiss something other than a hookah. We might be able to celebrate a double wedding!'

"I said double wedding because I was as sure of marrying Selina as I was certain we were poor.

"'Ah, Stavraki!' exclaimed the poor old man. 'You have a lot to learn about life!'

"He was a good prophet.

"Selina arrived. She was beautiful with brown devilish eyes and lots of hair. She was tall, solid, as quick as mercury, with the soul of a business-woman and the smarts of a harlot. She thanked us dryly and briefly for helping her mother. She found our lives disgusting, and came close to blaming us for her mother's misery. She expressed her disdain by renting a house for herself alone. When she deigned to visit, she only stayed fifteen minutes. The ridiculously little amount of money she turned over to Set Amra was supposed to be for us, for our trouble in tending to her mother. She wore exotic clothes and expensive jewelry, and when she walked through the streets envious eyes turned to her from all sides. One day a neighbor told us that a handsome young man had come in a car from Beirut to visit her. Selina, my betrothed, my promised bride!

"'Ah, Barba Yani, life is full of deceptions,' I said leaning on my friend's shoulder.

"'Didn't you already know that, Stavraki? If you didn't, you've learned it again. Get your *ibrik,* get mine, and the cups and things. We're moving on. The world is beautiful.

"We left, leaving Set Amra in tears. And for three months we wandered through the wonderful countryside around Mt. Lebanon. We drank water from its fresh streams and sold the Lebanese our inexhaustible salep.

"'Salep! Salep! Here come the salep sellers!'

"'Isn't it true, Stavraki? The world is beautiful.'

"'Oh, Barba Yani, you are so right!'

"The world is beautiful? Not really. It's a lie. All beauty comes from our hearts but only when our hearts are filled with joy. The day when there is no joy within us, the world becomes a cemetery. And my heart and Barba Yani's body are buried in the beautiful soil of Lebanon.

"One day, near Dlepta, a sudden and unexpected attack came over Barba Yani, and he fell face down, striking his head on a rock.

"'Barba Yani! Please Barba Yani! What are you doing? Are you sick?

"Barba Yani would never be among the sick again. I was the one who would endure sickness and suffering.

"The loss of Barba Yani left me with a wounded heart and soul. The memory of his dear friendship and the desire to find someone else, despite everything, led me a few years later to return to my native land. My hope was to find a human being whom I could love as I had loved Kyra and my mother and Barba Yani."

That, as you will remember, was the story of Stavro, the peddler.

Christopher Sawyer-Lauçanno

A Note on the Translation

Romain Rolland tells us in his introduction, "the man who wrote these lively pages only began to learn French seven years ago by reading our classics." What Rolland is suggesting is that Istrati, despite being a self-learner and non-native speaker of French, is a masterful writer in his acquired language. Clearly this is correct. His style and syntax are those of an accomplished French writer. He does not, however, write the literary French of the academy. His narrative is closer to the language of the streets, peppered with slang and with conversational locutions. This style has a distinct charm and definite authenticity, but does make translation, at times, somewhat difficult.

My goal was to translate *Kyra Kyralina* not just literally (which I did) but accurately. To me "accurately" meant that the tone, style and vivacity of Istrati's language should be as present in English as it was in French. In short, I wanted *Kyra Kyralina* to sound as if it had been written in English.

The problem was never with what Istrati was saying; rather the challenge was with how to render his phrasing in English with the same degree of veracity, punch and liveliness. At first I thought it best to try to recreate Istrati in an English more common to the United States in the mid-1920s, complete with expressions from that era. But there were enormous problems with this, not the least of which was that I am not familiar with American street language from seven or eight decades ago. Even when I could come up with language from the early part of the last century, these locutions often sounded quite dated (or even incomprehensible). I finally decided that the best course was to find contemporary equivalents for many of Istrati's colorful phrases. In doing so I took great pains to preserve the original sense in French while also creating a translation for our time.

On occasion I also found Istrati's phrasing and syntax slightly skewed from standard French. Tamara Ceban of the Universitatea Spiru Haret din Bucuresti, in an interesting article on the language in *Kyra Kyralina*, attributes these non-standard French expressions to Istrati thinking in Romanian but writing in French.* I decided not to call attention to these fairly insignificant modifications from standard usage and have rendered them smoothly in English.

An additional issue was Istrati's frequent use of foreign words and expressions. In the French text these words are usually footnoted. I chose not to use notes but simply to define these terms within the narrative so as not to interrupt the flow of language. Istrati's use of these foreign phrases was clearly a conscious choice. The multilingual Stavro (like the author) would have liberally used foreign expressions in his speech since these terms were as native to him as his own language. As such, these foreign phrases function as devices to create an authentic discourse. I have left all of these foreign words in the original, although in some cases I have modernized spellings to conform with current Turkish, Romanian or Greek practice. Similarly, I have modernized place names when necessary.

*Tamara Ceban, "La problématique de la traduction des oeuvres de Panaït Istrati a l'esprit orientale—ecrivain de la littérateur francophone." *Actes du Colloque International de l'Année Francophone Internationale*, Alexandria, Egypt March 12-15, 2006.

Panaït Istrati

Panaït Istrati (1884-1935) published the book for which he is best known, *Kyra Kyralina*, in 1923; it was an immediate sensation in Europe, and Istrati was recognized there as one of the great Modernists, a judgment which holds today. Although the book was twice translated into English in the 1920s, it never achieved in the United States the great success it enjoyed abroad and has since been largely forgotten.

In part, this may have been due to its subject matter, for *Kyra Kyralina* is a set of interlocking narratives concerning a young gay man in a world somewhat more liberal sexually—the late years of the Ottoman Empire—than was the United States at this point. *Time* magazine argued in 1926 that the book was not "for the general public, which takes unkindly to abnormality no matter how subtly treated." One might recall that even James Joyce's *Ulysses* was banned in the United States until 1933 because of what some considered objectionable language.

Istrati was born in Romania six years after it broke away from the Ottoman Empire. Ottoman culture, however, pervaded the new nation throughout the author's boyhood, and as a young man, he traveled extensively through the empire and lived briefly in Istanbul, then known as Constantinople. Deeply influenced by life in the Middle East, he set *Kyra Kyralina* in the 1850s, the waning years of the reign of Sultan Abdülaziz I, when Ottoman culture still retained much of its traditional quality. The narrative structure and tone are much indebted to Middle Eastern traditions as seen, for example, in *The Thousand and One Nights*.

Istrati wrote in French, and it was in Paris, deeply fascinated at the time with life in the Orient, that he achieved his first great success. *Kyra Kyralina* was the first in a series known collectively as the Adrien Zograffi accounts or cycle, comparable in ambition, scope and, many would claim, achievement, to Marcel Proust's *À la recherche du temps perdu*.

Istrati stood on the far left politically and was a passionate advocate for the Soviet Union until his travels there revealed such a wealth of persecution and oppression that he withdrew all support and, for a while, flirted with the nationalist Iron Guard in his homeland. Abandoned as a "Troskeyite" by former friends who remained enamored of the Stalinist state and disillusioned with the Iron Guard, Istrati found himself increasingly alone. He was simultaneously critical of the West and particularly capitalist economies, a fact which certainly did not endear him to conservative Americans any more than did his broad-mindedness and honesty in sexual matters.

Abandoned by friends and suffering from advanced tuberculosis, Istrati entered a Romanian sanatorium, where he died in 1935, a few months short of his fifty-first birthday. He is buried in Bucharest.